GUNSWIFT

B one Shattuck's brother-in-law had been m irdered in a gold robbery and his sister ha l died of grief. Four men had committed the robbery and Shattuck is determined to hu it them down. He resigns from the Texas Ra gers and sets off to find them. He soon dis overs that Bass Eccles, the ringleader an l the key to finding both the missing gold and the three others, is now in Yuma Prison. Shattuck must find a way to get into the prison and win Eccles' confidence – or die in the process.

GUNSWIFT

GUNSWIFT

by

Gordon D. Shirreffs

The Golden West Large Print Books
Long Preston, North Yorkshire,
BD23 4ND, England.

British Library Cataloguing In Publication Data.

Shirreffs, Gordon D.
   Gunswift.

   A catalogue record of this book is
   available from the British Library

   ISBN   978-1-84262-923-9 pbk

First published 1956 by Thomas Bouregy & Company, Inc.

Copyright © 1956 by Thomas Bouregy & Company, Inc.
Copyright renewed 1984 by Gordon D. Shirreffs.

Cover illustration © Michael Thomas

The moral right of the author has been asserted

Published in Large Print 2013 by arrangement with
Golden West Literary Agency

The Golden West Large Print is an imprint of Library Magna
Books Ltd.

Printed and bound in Great Britain by
T.J. (International) Ltd., Cornwall, PL28 8RW

CHAPTER ONE

The cold wind seemed to be sweeping all the way up from the Sonora border, driving sheets of sand across the Willcox road, battering mercilessly at the lone horseman heading west. Tumbleweeds rolled swiftly across the alkali flats. Some of them brushed against the legs of the stocky coyote dun, throwing him off stride. The man himself was as blocky as the dun, wind- and sand-burned, loose and easy in his saddle. His blue eyes were slitted against the gritty sheets that swept about him. The day before they had told him at Lordsburg that the storm was not yet in full swing, but he had shaken his head at their advice that he sit out the storm in Lordsburg where the beer was cold and the women of the cribs just the opposite.

He had left early that afternoon, causing much speculation among the bar idlers who watched him vanish into the dun world to the west. He was loco; on the run with a posse trailing him; he was after someone himself. The last was right. Boone Shattuck was after four men and he meant to kill all of them.

The dim yellow lights of Willcox winked through the storm at ten o'clock that night.

The wind still moaned across the flats. For the last ten miles he had given the dun its head, letting him pick hio way through the shifting, whirling veils of sand. Boone was sorry for the sturdy dun, but an unholy haste had driven him from Ysleta, the home station of A Company, Frontier Battalion, Texas Rangers. He had bought the dun at a corral in El Paso for a specific reason. Old-time Texas mustangers said, 'If you would lead the riders, pick the coyote dun.' Emilio Estrada, *cocinero* for A Company, had once told Boone, 'The bay dies while the dun will thrive wherever there is grass. The dun keeps cool amid difficulties that set the bay into a panic.' Old Emilio had been right.

Boone kneed the dun into the shelter of a ramshackle shed at the town's outskirts. He rolled a smoke, snapping a lucifer on his thumbnail to light it. The flickering light revealed the twisted white scar that ran from the corner of his left eye down to the edge of his mouth. He dragged deeply on the first smoke he had had since morning coffee and eyed the dusty street ahead of him. Lamplight showed through dirty cracked windows. Papers and tumbleweeds blew about the streets. The wind carried the offkey tinkling of a piano to him.

Boone dismounted and led the weary dun to a sagging livery stable. The liveryman sleepily showed him a stall and the oat bin.

Boone watered and fed his mount, rubbed him down and covered him with a blanket. He took his Winchester and saddlebags and stepped out into the windy darkness. A woman across the street, looking up and down the dismal thoroughfare, turned to walk toward the center of town.

'Lookit the filly, Cass,' a man said from the shadows beside the stable.

Boone stepped back into the doorway. Two men stepped out from the shadows and walked toward the young woman, swaying against the blast of the cold wind. One of them reached out and gripped her by the right arm. 'Hello, girlie. How's about a drink of forty-rod with me and Cass here?'

Cass lurched a little. 'Hellsfire, Billy!' he said. 'It's Jonce Maxon's daughter.'

Billy laughed. 'I'll be damned! Old drunken Jonce! Well, she shouldn't mind drinkin' with us then, Cass.'

The girl drew back but Billy hung on. Her left hand lashed out, cracking flatly against the drunk's face. Boone dropped his saddlebags and leaned his Winchester against the wall. He crossed toward the trio, freeing his tied-down Colt.

Boone stopped behind the short man. 'That's enough, Billy,' he said.

'What the hell?' said Billy. He released the girl, swaying as he turned, and threw a looping right at Boone. Boone blocked the blow and clipped Billy against the jaw with a right hook. Billy reeled backward.

Cass cursed and slapped his hand down for a draw. Boone freed his Colt and slapped the heavy barrel alongside Cass's head, just below the hatbrim. The lanky man went down without a sound. Billy rushed in, tripped over his partner's legs and went down. Boone kicked out. The high bootheel caught Billy just behind the left ear.

Boone holstered his Colt. 'Are you all right, Miss Maxon?'

'Yes.' She looked down at the two unconscious men. 'How did you know my name?'

'I heard Brother Cass say you were Jonce Maxon's daughter.'

'I'm Marion Maxon. I was looking for my father.'

'I'll take you to him.'

She eyed him for a moment. 'All right.'

Boone picked up his saddlebags and rifle.

A tall, loose-jointed man came out of a saloon and wiped his mouth. He swayed a little as he stepped out into the street. 'There's Father now,' she said as she stopped. Yellow light from a store window flooded Boone's face, revealing the lean planes, the twisted scar and the light blue eyes, startling in the deeply tanned face. Her eyes widened and she involuntarily drew back. 'I don't even know your name.'

'Boone. Boone Shattuck, Miss Marion.'

'Thanks. Thanks for helping me.' She hurried toward the drunken man and helped him across the wind-blasted street.

Boone had a clear impression of hazel eyes, a soft-looking mouth and fine clear skin. An oval face, framed in light brown hair and a perky bonnet. He shrugged and trudged toward the nearest saloon.

Boone pushed through the sagging doors and placed his saddlebags on a chair near the door, leaning his rifle beside it. He took off his gray hat and slapped the dust from his clothing. A dozen men were in the place. Hazy tobacco smoke lifted and wavered in cross drafts from ill-fitting doors and windows. A huge cast-iron stove stood at the back of the room. Coal-oil harp lamps swayed from their cords.

Boone walked to the end of the long bar and called for a beer. The fat bartender waddled down to him and placed the glass on the bar. 'You just come in offa the road?' he asked curiously. Boone nodded. Several men looked up at him.

The bartender shook his head. 'Last year two *hombres* started out from Tombstone, coming up this way, in a storm as bad as this one. They was found a week later near Dos Cabezas. Dead as doornails. Ain't no time to ride the road, brother.'

'I'm lucky,' said Boone dryly.

Wind scrabbled at the walls. A door banged

11

somewhere in the rear rooms. The bartender waddled down to the far end of the bar and said something in a low voice to a man standing there. The man nodded.

Boone rolled a smoke and leaned against the bar. Jim Dobie, Wells-Fargo detective in that district, was supposed to meet him in Willcox. All Boone knew about Dobie was that he was a top man, short and stocky, with reddish hair and green eyes.

The front door banged open. The strong draft swept cards from a table. One of the players cursed and looked up angrily at the tall newcomer, then looked hastily away. The light glinted dully on a badge pinned to his loud-checked coat. He wiped his black dragoon mustache both ways. Cold eyes settled on Boone. 'You,' he said. 'You just come in?'

The soft slap of cards and the click of chips died away. A man coughed nervously.

'Yes,' Boone said.

'I'm Bob Dowling, city marshal. I got a complaint from two citizens.'

'You mean those two drunks who were annoying a young woman?'

'They didn't say anything about that.'

'Maybe you'd better ask them.'

Dowling tried to stare down Boone. 'Billy Steen got a helluva wallop,' he said.

'He's lucky.'

The door opened behind Dowling. He

whirled and stepped back against the wall like a great lean cat. Cass came in, holding the side of his head. 'That's him, Bob,' he said.

'I'll have to take you in to the calabozo, stranger,' said Dowling.

'On what charge?'

'Assault and battery.'

'The Territory is changin',' Boone said quietly. He eyed Cass. 'Used to be the local boys would ride a bum like this out of town for annoyin' a lady.'

A big red-faced man looked up from a table. 'He's right there, Dowling,' he said.

Dowling looked about the room. There was no friendship in the eyes that met his. It was obvious that he was feared and hated by all the men in the saloon.

'Forget it, Bob,' said Cass.

'He'd better,' said the big man.

Cass fingered the lump beneath his hat-brim. 'Billy and me can handle him in our own way.'

The bartender grinned. 'Looks like he can handle hisself all right. Ain't no marks on *him*, Cass.'

'Shut up, Fatty! You talk too damned much!' Cass whirled and left the saloon.

Dowling reached for a bottle of rye, drank deeply and then wiped his mustache. 'You're a stranger,' he said quietly. 'Now you listen to me! I'm the law here in Willcox! You keep

13

your nose clean or I won't let you off so easy next time!'

'I hear you,' said Boone.

The marshal's eyes flicked down toward the Colt. 'Remember, then.' He left the saloon.

The bartender wiped the mouth of the bottle. 'Bastard never *does* pay for a drink,' he said.

Boone shoved his beer glass forward. 'Regular bull of the woods, eh?'

'Yeh. Mean as a Nueces *ladino*. Spends most of his time beatin' up the hurdy-gurdy girls and rollin' drunks.'

Fatty filled the beer glass. 'Some of the boys call him the Fighting Pimp. Just you keep outa his way, mister. Watch out for Caston and Steen. They was drunk tonight, and they don't believe in turnin' the other cheek.'

'*Gracias!* Where's the hotel?'

'The beer is on me. The hotel, such as it is, is half a block up. On the corner. None of us here like Dowling, Caston and Steen any better'n you do. They're hard case. Useta run around with Bass Eccles!'

'That mean anything?' Boone asked.

The barkeep looked up and down the bar. 'For sure he's a stranger! Never heard of Bass Eccles?'

Boone had. Eccles was one of the quartet he was after. 'Nice town you have here,' he said. 'With men like them runnin' about.'

14

'Oh, it ain't the *town!* It's some of the people in it that makes it what it is.'

Boone nodded. He drained his glass and left the saloon. He walked through the darkness to the two-story hotel, checked in and climbed wearily to his room.

Boone locked his door and stripped to the waist to clean up. A puckered bullet hole showed at the base of his left ribs. He cleaned up and pulled on a fresh undershirt. He placed his Colt beneath the pillow and rolled a smoke. He lowered the lamp and dropped on the hard bed.

Eight months ago the news had come to him while on a scout in the Sierra Tinaja that Perry Thorne had died in a railway holdup ten miles west of Willcox near Cochise Junction while serving as a Wells-Fargo guard in the express car. Three men had done the job, stopping the train eight miles from Willcox and uncoupling the express car from the rest of the cars. They had forced the engineer to draw the lone car two miles farther west. Perry had been buffaloed into unconsciousness. The bandits had attempted to open the safe, set with a time lock. When they had failed they had set a charge of blasting powder which had lifted the top clear off the car. Forty thousand dollars' worth of mint gold, consigned to Los Angeles from Denver, had been the haul.

Boone stared up at the dim ceiling. Perry

Thorne had been left unconscious in the car before the blast. A few bloody rags pasted to the shattered woodwork of the car had been the only trace found of him. Boone had immediately asked for a leave of absence from the Rangers. Sergeant Tobe Winkler had told him to finish the scout after Sixto Escobar, a pure quill *ladrone* from Chihuahua. In the fight Boone had killed Escobar but had been dropped with a fifty-caliber slug through the body. The last round in Boone's six-gun had dropped the outlaw after he had raked Boone's face from eye to mouth with a razor-edged *cuchillo*. The wounds had kept him in an El Paso hospital for six months while the trail in Arizona had grown cold.

Boone closed his eyes. His sister Emilie, cute as a button, Perry Thorne's wife, had not even recognized Boone when she had been taken to the hospital to see him. The vacant look in her blue eyes often haunted him at night. She had been Boone's last living blood relative until she had died during the winter.

Boone reached into his saddlebags and took out a bottle of rye. He drank deeply and felt the liquor soak into his body. His resignation from A Company had gone through. His recommendation had gained him an appointment as a special Wells-Fargo detective. Phil Mason, chief of the district, had been glad to get him.

Mason had briefed him on the unsolved case. Dance Younger had been seen flashing freshly minted twenty dollar gold pieces in Benson shortly after the holdup. Then he had vanished. Sim Bellam's voice had been recognized by the engineer as one of the three masked men. Bartolome Huerta, a coldblooded *bandido* from Sonora, had been seen with both men the day before the holdup, buying blasting powder at the old Acme mine. All three men had ridden into Willcox at midnight with Bass Eccles, one-time city marshal of Willcox. Bass had sworn all three men had been drinking with him all day long in his adobe two miles west of town. But Mason, as well as many other lawmen, was sure Eccles had engineered the whole deal. None of the gold, other than that spent by Younger in Benson, had ever been found.

Boone took another drink. He didn't give a fiddler's damn about the stolen gold. He wanted to put the fear of death into the eyes of those four men, Eccles, Younger, Bellam and Huerta, before he killed them.

CHAPTER TWO

Boone suddenly sat up in bed. The room was cold. The wind rattled the warped window casing. He listened. Something seemed to have warned him. He took out his Colt and padded restlessly about the room, wary as a lobo wolf. He snapped open the cover of his repeater watch. After midnight. He sat down at the little table and drew his saddlebags close. He took out his cleaning materials and set to work on his Colt. Cleaning his weapons always seemed to calm him.

He had finished with his Colt and was working on his double-barreled derringer when he heard a stairstep creak. He stood up and cocked his Colt. Someone was in the hall, just beyond the thin door.

A soft tap hit the door. Boone did not move. The tap was repeated. 'Shattuck!' a man whispered hoarsely. 'It's Dobie! Jim Dobie! Open up!'

Boone reached across, unlocked the door and eased it partway open. 'Come in with your hands up!' he said.

A short, well-built man, pushed through the doorway with his hands resting atop his hat. Humorous green eyes surveyed Boone.

'Suspicious *hombre,* ain't you?'

'I've lived thirty years by being suspicious.'

'Can I take my hands down now?'

'Easy like. Where's your credentials?'

'In my left boot.'

'Set and pull it off.'

Boone shut the door and locked it as Dobie sat down and removed the boot. He fished his badge and identification out of it and showed it to Boone. 'Fair enough.'

Dobie replaced them in his boot and pulled it on.

'Drink?' asked Boone.

'After I see *your* badge.'

Boone grinned, took the badge and paper out of the inner pocket of his trousers. Dobie nodded, crossed to the window and drew down the tattered shade. 'I heard a mean lookin' stranger got into a hassle a couple of hours ago.' He eyed Boone. 'You?'

'Yes. Two drunks bothered a young woman.'

'Jesus! Billy Steen and Cass Caston. It didn't take you long to get into trouble.'

'They don't know who I am.'

Dobie scaled his hat at a hook and watched it settle and swing back and forth. 'In this business, Shattuck, we don't *look* for trouble.'

'I didn't agree to let a lady get molested and stand by when I signed up with Wells-Fargo.'

'It was a damned fool thing to do!'

19

The cold blue eyes held Dobie's green ones. 'You didn't come here to talk about that, did you?'

For a moment Dobie looked as though he was going to get riled and then he looked at the bottle. 'I'll have that drink now, Shattuck. Damned near forgot you were a Texas man.'

Boone filled glasses and dropped into a chair.

'You're a marked man in Willcox now,' said Dobie.

Boone touched the scar on his lean face. 'I've been marked for some time,' he said dryly.

'What did Mason tell you and where the hell have you been?'

Boone drained his glass. 'I'll answer the last question first. I rode in from El Paso.'

'With the train available?'

Boone nodded. 'Everyone watches a man who gets off a train in a small town like this. No one worries much about a lone horseman.'

'True enough.'

'I would have been here months ago except a Mex *ladrone* nearly cashed in my chips for me.'

Dobie nodded. 'Perry Thorne was your brother-in-law, wasn't he?'

'As well as my best friend.'

Dobie lit a cigar. 'I really didn't want you on this case. This is a ticklish business. I wanted a cool man who isn't driving himself because of the murder of his brother-in-law.'

Boone leaned forward. *'Let's get this straight, once and for all!* Mason thinks I'm qualified. I was told to work with you. I'm willing to. I want to get the four men who did the job. If some of them are gunned down in the process, so much the better!'

Dobie inspected his cigar. 'I've done too damned much work on this case to have a gunfighter mess it up.'

'Just don't get any ideas that you'll notify Mason I won't do for the job. I'll promise you that you'll be satisfied.'

Dobie eyed the man watching him. A cold finger seemed to trace the line of his spine as he looked at the lean scarred face, almost as though Death were eyeing him speculatively 'All right, Shattuck,' he said, 'you win. I'll take your word on it.'

Boone nodded and refilled the glasses. 'Bring me up to date.'

'I relieved Johnny Bascomb two months ago. He had been recognized. I've never worked this territory before. I didn't do a helluva lot the first month. Just lazed around town, showing just enough money to let people know I was fairy well heeled. I've located Younger.'

Boone's head jerked up. 'So?'

'He has a small spread near the Swisshelms making out like he's an honest rancher.'

The wind rattled the window casing.

'Bellam has been seen in Gila Bend, Prescott, Globe and lately in and around Rustler's Canyon.'

'What about Huerta?'

'He's in Nacozari, down in Sonora, about seventy-five miles south of the border. One of our men went down there. He never came back.'

'What about Bass Eccles?'

Dobie picked a piece of tobacco from his lip. 'All we have on him is the fact that he engineered alibis for the other three. He's never really been connected with the robbery.'

'What do you think?'

'None of the three who robbed the car has enough brains to pound sand down a rathole They're rough as cobs and are killers, but stupid. Eccles is shrewd. It'd be like him to plan a big haul like that and keep his shirttail out of the manure. My God, Shattuck! Forty thousand in gold can't just vanish in this country! Dance Younger had only a few gold-pieces. We know Bellam is broke. Huerta never flashed any of the gold.'

'Eccles seems to have quite a reputation around here.'

'Yeh. An odd duck. Used to be city marshal here. Before that he was deputy-sheriff of Cochise County. Has the reputation of a killer. When he left his job here he got mixed

22

up with a border gang of hardcase Americans and Mexes. Rustling, stealing and a little high-grading. Seems as though Eccles has some high-placed *amigos* who keep their mouths shut and give him a hand now and then.'

'Where is he now?'

'Are you familiar with Arizona?'

'I was a mulepacker with Crook back in the early 80s.'

Dobie looked at Boone with new respect. Crook's mulepackers had been hand-picked men, fighters and scouts as well as nurses for their flop-eared charges.

'Do I pass?' asked Boone.

'You'll do.' Dobie scratched his jaw. 'Eccles and his three sidekicks came into town about midnight and went on a hell-roarin' drunk. When the sheriff questioned Younger, Bellam and Huerta, Eccles swore they had been with him all day. What could be done? They were in the clear and, by God, no one around here was going to call Bass Eccles a liar.'

'You didn't tell me where he was.'

'In Yuma Pen. Serving time.'

Boone's head snapped up. 'What for?'

'Attempted robbery of a stagecoach near Pearce. Bungled the job after wounding the shotgun messenger slightly. A passenger got the drop on him and he lost his nerve. He got a year.'

'Can't he be made to talk?'

'Bass Eccles? Hell no!'

'When does he get out?'

'In about five weeks. He got several months off for good behavior.'

'We could wait for him to get out and then shadow him.'

Dobie wet his lips. 'You think he wouldn't know about it?'

'You *said* he was shrewd.'

'He is. I've always suspected that he bungled that stagecoach robbery just to get put into the calabozo.'

Boone eyed the detective. 'What do you mean?'

'He's safe enough in there from his old friends.'

'I don't follow you.'

'Simple. I think Eccles knows where that mint gold is. I think he double-crossed his three *companeros* and then got sent to Yuma to be safe from them.'

'It's a long shot, Dobie.'

'Mebbeso, but you couldn't put a deal like that past Eccles.'

'So what does he gain? They'd be waitin' for him when he gets out.'

'Yeh. *If they knew when he was getting out.*'

The wind moaned about the rumshackle hotel. Sand scrabbled at the warped wooden walls. Boone rolled a smoke. Dobe stood up. 'I said he had friends. Supposing he was let out at a time when no one suspected when it would be?'

Boone drew smoke deep into his lungs. 'You think it can be done?'

'*Quien sabe?* Some years ago Bass was mixed up in the Tucson Ring. A gang of politicians, contractors and traders who worked machine politics to line their pockets. Selling whiskey and firearms to the Apaches. Their policy was to prevent the Apaches from becoming self-supporting so that the Ring could make profits by selling supplies to the government for them. The Indian Bureau had members who worked hand in glove with the Ring by confiscating crops, moving the tribes to barren reservations and then shifting them again when precious metals were found on land supposedly not worth a damn! Many of the members of the Ring have become respectable after making their stake. Some of them are old *companeros* of Eccles, now in responsible territorial positions.'

Boone nodded.

Dobie crushed out his cigar. 'Besides, every damned lawman in the Territory would like to trail Eccles to that hidden gold. Sheriffs, U.S. Marshals, Pinkertons and what have you.'

'You forgot Wells-Fargo.'

'No I didn't! They're angling for the reward. Our job is to get that bullion back for

25

the company.'

Boone eyed the stocky detective. 'A company man, eh?'

'Supposing an outlaw made fools of the Texas Rangers?'

'Few do, if any.'

'Yes. You'd make damned sure the stain was wiped off the name of the Texas Rangers, wouldn't you? Well, Shattuck, I feel the same way about Wells-Fargo!'

Boone stood up. 'Supposing we planted a man in Yuma?'

'It's been tried. Eccles is slick as a greased pig.'

'It's worth another try.'

'We could get a man in, all right.'

Boone looked at him. 'Let me go.'

'If he gets wise, you'll never leave Yuma alive.'

'I'll take that chance.'

'Let me think about it.'

'Don't think too long.'

Dobie eyed Boone. 'Who are you supposed to be?'

'Saddlebum. Drifter.'

'You look tough enough to go to Yuma, with that scar.'

'Thanks.'

'No offense.'

'Forget it.'

'I still don't like it.'

'Let *me* worry about it.'

'Eccles is a killer. Fast as greased lightning and eleven claps of thunder with a six-gun.'

'I can take care of myself.'

'*If* you get out of Yuma with him. It will take planning.'

'Where can I contact you here in town?'

'I'm working as jailor. Best place to pick up information.'

'I don't know of a better.'

'Sheriff Kelly is a good man. He's been working with me. I'll contact him to see what we can do.' Dobie put on his hat. 'Meanwhile, keep out of trouble.'

'What else could I have done tonight?'

'I suppose I would have done the same. Still, it makes things difficult.'

Boone unlocked the door. 'Who is Jonce Maxon?'

'Rancher. Has a spread near Pearce. Why?'

'It was Marion Maxon who was mauled by those two drunks.'

Dobie whistled softly. 'Maxon used to be a friend of Eccles years ago. They were deputy-sheriffs together. Eccles used to spend a lot of time at Maxon's place. I've heard a rumor that Jonce might have been mixed up in the robbery.'

'Seems as though a lot of people were.'

Dobie nodded. 'Well, pleasant dreams, Shattuck.'

Boone peeled off his clothing and crawled into bed. A picture formed in his mind of

Perry Thorne. Somehow the picture faded just before he dropped off to sleep, replaced by an oval face and hazel eyes beneath the brim of a perky bonnet.

CHAPTER THREE

The wind had died away during the night and the sun showed through a dull haze. Boone dressed quickly and swung his gunbelt about his waist.

He thought of Billy Steen and Cass Caston and took his hideout gun from a saddlebag. It was a round-handled Colt double-action. Gus Schmidt of El Paso had converted it into a belly gun by shortening the original seven-and-a-half inch barrel to two inches, cutting off the hammer spur, and removing the front of the trigger guard. Boone slipped the stingy gun into his left coat pocket and left.

The hazy sun revealed the warped and faded buildings of Willcox in all their ugliness. Boone stopped at a small beanery for breakfast. A young woman sat at a corner table, her dress bedraggled and her tawdry hat hanging to one side of her head. She hiccupped as Boone glanced at her and returned his look with a stare of pure hatred. A purplish bruise showed beneath her swollen left eye.

The waitress served Boone his breakfast, eyeing him curiously. She was a plump girl with amazingly big blue eyes. 'You're new in town, ain'tcha?'

Boone nodded.

'Travelin' through or stayin'?'

'*Quien sabe?* I might look about a bit.'

'Texan, ain'tcha?'

Boone glanced at her in amusement. 'Yes.'

She poured herself a cup of coffee. 'My name is Lily. Some of the boys call me The Jersey Lily although I ain't never been in New Jersey in my life.'

Boone grinned. 'They mean Lily Langtry. She's from Jersey in England.'

The girl raised her eyebrows. 'Yeh? What is she? Hurdy-gurdy girl? Monte dealer? Hash-slinger?'

'Actress. A beautiful woman.'

'Well, I'll be damned! All the time I thought the boys was ribbing me.'

'They weren't. There's a town named after Lily down in Texas. Langtry. Not far from where the Pecos meets the Rio Grande.'

'Sure enough? Well, I never!'

'Lily!' It was the battered girl at the table.

'Comin', honey!' The waitress bustled over to the girl. 'You want I should put some beefsteak on that eye?'

'To hell with it!' the woman said. 'I'll wear

29

this damned bruise until it fades away! I'll show Bob Dowling!'

Lily patted her shoulder. 'You just sit tight. I'll get more coffee.'

'To hell with it! Give me some whiskey.'

'Now, Nelly! You know I don't serve rotgut. I'll get some coffee. Then you can lie down in my room for awhile.'

The waitress came back to the counter and filled a cup. She leaned toward Boone. 'She's from the cribs,' she said in a low voice. 'Bob Dowling beat her up early this morning.'

'Nice fella.'

She drew back her lips. 'Him? Swaggers around town like God. Beats up the hurdy-gurdy girls. Second time in a month he worked over Nelly there.'

Boone looked at the battered prostitute. She couldn't be more than twenty years old.

The waitress glanced out the window. 'Here comes the skunk now.'

Nelly's head jerked. She touched her bruised face.

Lily balled her fists. 'He ain't gonna bother yuh, honey.'

'Keep out of it, Lily,' she said quietly.

The door banged open and Bob Dowling swaggered in. Boone turned on his stool and rested his elbows on the counter. Bob glanced at the girl and then at Boone. 'Get back to the house,' he said.

Lily raised her head. 'She's resting here, Bob.'

'Yeh? I told you before to keep your big nose outa my business, Lily.'

Lily eyed him. 'I ain't ascared of you, Bob Dowling.'

'Maybe you'll get a little of what Nelly got.'

She laughed. 'You lay a hand on me, you ugly galoot, and my brother will come a-lookin' for you.'

'I'm worried.'

'Yuh better be.'

Boone shifted. Dowling turned partway toward him. There was a naked challenge in his smoldering eyes.

Lily helped the half-drunken girl to her feet. 'The bed is fresh made,' she said. 'You can stay as long as yuh like.'

Dowling reached out a big hairy hand. Boone stood up. The marshal eyed him. 'She started a ruckus this morning in the Acme.'

'Let her alone,' Boone said.

'I've got to fine her.'

'How much?'

'Ten dollars.'

Boone took two fives from his shirt pocket and threw them on the table. Boone jerked his head at Lily. 'Put her to bed.'

Dowling picked up the bills. 'You aimin' to stay long in Willcox?'

31

'I might.'

'I warned you once last night. This is the second time. There won't be a third.'

Dowling turned on a heel and left the beanery. The building shook with the impact of the slamming door.

The big waitress came back into the room. 'That ornery, stinkin', no-good scum,' she said. 'You should see Nelly's back.'

Boone smacked a fist into his other palm.

'Yeh. I feel that way, too. Dowling takes a cut from the hurdy-gurdy joints. He takes another cut from the girls. He beats them up and then fines them for disorderly conduct.'

'A real bloodsucker.'

'You said it. But he's leery of my brother. Say! You must be the fella he told me about. The *hombre* that beat up Billy Steen and Cass Caston.'

'Your brother?'

'*Muy hombre!* A big man. Red face.'

'I think I saw him last night. Wearing a gray coat and black hat.'

'That's him. Eli Bell. Bob don't fool with Eli, I tell you.'

Boone paid for his meal. 'I'm glad somebody stands up to him.'

'Eli don't get along with Bob. They useta be friends about a year ago. Ever since Bass Eccles got jugged in Yuma last year, Bob has been gettin' worse and worse. Had a falling out with Eli, too.'

'Why would the jailing of Bass Eccles make Bob proddy? Were they *amigos?*'

'Useta be. Eli thinks Bass double-crossed Bob on that express robbery last year. You hear about that?'

'A little.'

'Folks say Bass hid that gold and Bob was supposed to have got some of it.'

'You believe that?'

She snorted. 'Why, Bass, Dance Younger, Sim Bellam and Bartolome Huerta was in here the morning after the robber. Been goin' the town all night. They spent the day before out at Eccles' 'dobe, two miles west of here. I never believed Bass was in on it. Bass and me was sweethearts then. Bass woulda told me, don't you think?'

Boone eyed the buxom girl. 'How could he have kept it back?'

She flushed. 'You see?'

'Anybody living in Eccles' place now?'

'Not since he got jugged.'

Boone walked toward the jail. Jim Dobie was seated on a bench in front of it. Boone nodded. Dobie looked up and down the quiet street. 'Castor and Steen are in the Acme talking war,' he said. 'Take off for awhile.'

'I figured I might take a look at Eccles' adobe.'

'Fair enough. Follow the road west about

two miles. The 'dobe is about half a mile north of the road. You won't find anything out there.'

'Who knows? See you later.'

Boone crossed to the livery stable and saddled his dun. He led it behind the hotel and went up to his room to get his Winchester. He headed north out of town, looking back now and then to see if anyone was behind him.

The flats were deserted.

CHAPTER FOUR

Boone topped a rise to look down on a squat adobe set in a wide hollow. He drew rein, eyeing the structure below him.

One end of the roof had sagged in. The area about the house was littered with wood, rusty tin cans and bits of glass, tinted purple and red by the hot sun. A ramshackle shed leaned against one end of the adobe. The remains of a fence leaned every which way, surrounding about half an acre behind the house. A peeled-pole corral had been partially torn down.

Boone kneed the dun down the slope and ground-reined in behind the house. The front door sagged on leather hinges. He pulled it back to enter the low-ceilinged living room. The accumulated odors of human waste clung about him. Battered furniture stood about. Ashes were thick in the beehive fireplace in a corner. Glass crunched under his boots. It looked as though no one had lived there for a long time.

Boone picked up a stick and lifted a tattered, filthy blanket from the floor. A dirty shirt was beneath it. He walked into a smaller room. Sunlight streamed through the narrow windows. A scrawled message was on one wall, written with charcoal. Boone read it aloud:

'Within this hive we're all alive,
Good whiskey makes us funny;
So if you're dry come up and try
The flavor of our honey.'

Boone grinned. The room was empty except for a fallen cot. He lifted it and looked underneath. A mouse scuttled for cover.

Boone walked into the filthy kitchen. A rusted stove was place against the back wall and the pipes had collapsed across it, littering the stove and floor with soot. A woodbox, partially filled, stood beside it.

He walked out the back door to inspect the shed. A broken saddle hull hung from a peg. Straw still covered the hard earth floor.

Boone walked back to the house. The dun

whinnied softly and thrust forward its ears, looking to the east, toward the lip of the hollow. Boone stepped into the house, crossed into the living room and stood back from a window watching the mesquite along the hollow edge. It did not move.

Boone leaned against the wall and eyed the big room. He was wasting time, he knew. Forty thousand in gold would be compact but damned heavy. He was willing to bet Keno, his dun against a chew of spit-or-drown that the gold couldn't have been hauled far from the robbery before it was cached. Mint gold was carried in small wooden boxes, sealed with wax. Boone had once acted as guard on an express train which carried twenty thousand in gold. There had been two boxes. Therefore each box must have contained ten thousand dollars. By that line of reasoning, there must have been four boxes removed from the Southern Pacific express car by the three outlaws. A real bonanza!

Boone walked back into the kitchen and poked about in the old stove. It was deep in ashes. He dumped the woodbox over and pawed through it. Suddenly he whistled. The bottom of the box was stained with melted wax. He took out his case knife and scraped at it. It was thick. Odds were that the heat of the stove, close to the woodbox, had melted the wax. But where had it come from? It was reddish. Certainly not candle wax. 'I'll be go-to-hell,' he said.

He refilled the woodbox, carefully examining each piece. One piece had been split in half. It was half an inch thick. There was a dark stain on one end. He scraped at it with his knife and tasted the scrapings. Wax! He stowed the piece of wood in his coat pocket and left the adobe.

He led Keno toward the lip of the hollow, topped it and stopped short. There were six shallow marks in the loose sand. He squatted, measuring them with his eye. A man, lying prone on his belly, would have made just such hollows with elbows, knees and boot toes. Two hundred yards from the hollow he found hoofmarks. They had not been there when he had passed by earlier.

Boone swung up on the dun and headed back toward Willcox. He rode slowly. Melted wax was no real clue. Yet it was a lead...

A tall man sat in a buckboard at the edge of town, looking down the long dusty street. He jumped as he heard Keno's hoofs on the hard earth. He turned and eyed Boone with red-rimmed eyes. Boone nodded.

'You're Boone Shattuck, ain't you?' the man asked.'

'Yes.'

The tall man passed a shaking hand across his forehead. 'I'm Jonce Maxon. Marion tells me you did her a kindness last night when she was lookin' for me.'

'It was nothing,' said Boone. Maxon's face was livery in color. Pouches hung below the red eyes. He had all the marks of a steady drinker. He had been a fine-looking, powerful man in his day, but the shakes had taken over.

Maxon steadied his hands. 'Yeh. *Nothing,* he says.'

Maxon's tone wasn't that of a grateful man.

'I don't get it, Maxon.'

'You think I want Steen and Caston on the prod after me? I got troubles enough as it is.'

'Maybe I should have let them rough her up?'

'She woulda been all right!' Maxon wet his purplish lips. 'Looky here, son. I appreciate what you done, all right. Years ago I woulda done the same thing for any lady. But I was a better man then. I been sick.'

Boone studied the raddled face. 'You sure as hell are.'

Maxon flushed. 'Likker helps me along. Drives away the pains.'

'So?'

Maxon swallowed. 'I'm gettin' out of town back to my ranch before them two bastards come lookin' for me like they are for you. It's your fight. They give me a hard time some months ago. I ain't hankerin' to get it again.'

Maxon threaded the reins through his gnarled fingers. 'You wouldn't happen to have a bottle on you, would you?'

'No.'

Maxon looked uneasily up the street. 'I told that girl to meet me here at noon!'

Boone touched the dun with his spurs. 'I'll see if I can find her for you.'

'Much obliged.'

A woman was standing near the hotel looking up and down the street. The wind blew her dress flat against her long shapely legs and taut against her full breasts. Boone tethered the dun to a hitching rack.

She smiled as she saw him. 'Good morning.'

'It *is* a good morning. Your father is waiting for you at the edge of town.'

'Thanks, Mister Shattuck.'

'The name is Boone.'

'Boone.'

Boone took off his hat. 'I'll walk you to him.'

'Thank you. He hasn't been well. I brought him in to see Doctor Ruffin but Dad refused to see him last night. I just can't get him to see a doctor.'

She took Boone's arm as they walked. 'How do you like Willcox?' she asked.

'What is there to like about Willcox?'

She laughed. 'You have me there. I like the ranch much better. Run down as it is, it's much more peaceful and clean.'

A woman eyed them from the doorway of

39

a general store and then spoke over her shoulder to a man who stood behind her. They followed Marion and Boone with their eyes as they passed. Marion flushed. 'Will you stay here long?'

'I'm passin' through.'

'Cowman?'

'A little. Cowpoke, mulepacker, scout, drifter.'

'A Texan.'

'Yes.'

'You've a family in Texas?' She glanced at him.

Boone shook his head. 'I'm the last of my family. The last of my line of the Shattucks.'

'That sounds so final. *The last of the Shattucks.*'

'My father was killed by Comanches at Horsehead Crossing on the Pecos when I was a kid. My mother died of fever shortly after that. My brother Collate was drowned in the Solomon River, north of Abilene, on a trail drive. My kid sister … she died last year.'

'Texas must be a hard country.'

'In a way. Old-timers say it's a fine country for men and dogs, but hell on women and horses.'

Jonce Maxon was standing up on the floor of the buckboard watching them from two blocks away. A man stepped out of a saloon and started toward Maxon, saw Marion and Boone, and hurriedly stepped between two buildings. It was Cass Caston. Boone unbuttoned his coat.

'There's Father,' said Marion.

Maxon touched up his teams and rode slowly toward them.

Billy Steen came out of the saloon and stood beneath the wooden awning. Suddenly he crossed the street in front of them and stopped in front of a blacksmith shop. Boone saw what they were up to. He would have to walk between them to take the girl to her father. *Why didn't the drunken fool hurry?*

Fifty yards from the buckboard, Caston stepped out into the open. The wind flopped open his gaudy cowhide vest. Marion paled. 'Keep walking,' said Boone.

'Will there be trouble?'

'If anything happens, you drop to the ground and stay there. Do you understand?'

'Yes. But they have guns.'

He grinned. 'Why ... so have I.'

Maxon reined in the team and looked nervously from Steen to Caston and then at Boone and the girl. 'Hurry, Marion!' he called.

Billy Steen stepped out into the street. 'You!' he said to Boone. 'I want to talk to you.'

Boone stopped. 'Let the lady go to her father,' he said.

Steen glanced across the street. Caston leaned against a post. Steen swept back his

41

coat from his left side. His right hand shot across his squat body for a cross-arm draw. Boone smashed against the girl, driving her to the hard earth. Steen fired. The crack of the Colt sounded loudly in the stillness. The slug sang thinly past Boone's head. He jumped away from the girl, ripping his Colt free of leather. Caston ran forward.

'Look out, Boone!' screamed Marion.

Boone whirled. Caston slammed his long-barrelled Colt down across Boone's gun wrist. Boone grunted in agony, dropping his six-gun, and swung from the waist, driving a vicious left to Caston's bristly jaw. Caston staggered sideways as Steen fired again. The cowhide vest jerked and dust flew from it. Caston pitched forward, gripping his lean gut.

Steen yelled through the wreathing smoke and started forward. He glanced down at Boone's fallen Colt and grinned. Boone sidled away. Steen ran forward, thrusting out his Colt.

Boone cleared his hide-out gun from his coat pocket and rapped out three staccato shots. The echoes slammed back and forth between the false-fronted buildings. Steen staggered backward, dropping his pistol. Then he pitched sideways, fell heavily, twitched spasmodically and lay still. Blood spread swiftly across the front of his white shirt.

Maxon peered through the rifting smoke. 'By God!' he said. 'He got both of 'em!' He jumped from the buckboard, gripped Marion by the arm, dragged her to her feet and shoved her toward the buckboard. As she sat down, he gripped the reins, slapped the whip across the dusty rumps of the team and turned the buckboard swiftly, racing off to the west. Marion Maxon looked back and then covered her face with her hands.

A crowd began to gather. An aproned clerk looked down at Caston. 'His tack is drove,' he said.

A cowman bent over Billy Steen. 'Three slugs in the gut,' he said over his shoulder. 'Yuh could cover them holes with the palm of your hand.' He stood up and looked at Boone in awe. 'Somebody better get marshal Dowling.'

Boone wiped the cold sweat from his face. It had happened so quickly he hadn't had time to think. He had done just what Dobie had warned him not to.

Dowling came up the street, his nickel-plated Colt glinting in his hand. The crowd gave way before him. 'I warned you, Shattuck,' he said. Before Boone could move, the marshal swung his heavy Colt. The long barrel clipped Boone over the left ear, driving him to his knees. The second blow caught him atop the head. He fought with reeling senses to get up. Dowling lashed out with a big booted foot. The heel hit Boone on the temple.

He struck the hard ground and lay still, knowing nothing.

CHAPTER FIVE

Boone opened his eyes and a ray of sunlight lanced deeply into his throbbing skull. He turned away from the window. He was in a cell. He sat up, wincing as pain shot through his battered head. He groaned softly.

'You sure as hell drove everything up the spout,' said a dry voice.

Boone looked up. Jim Dobie was looking through the bars at him. 'Kill two men in two minutes! Where the hell did you think you were? In some Mex *plazita* along the Rio Grande after some *ladrones?*'

'Shut up.'

'You acted like a whiskey fool out there.'

Boone gripped the bars and pulled himself to his feet. 'Where's Dowling?'

'Over at Doc Ruffin's at the autopsy. The fat is in the fire now.'

Boone suddenly thrust a hand into his inner pocket.

'I got your badge and papers out when they carried you in here. I'm sending them

44

back to Mason with a request that he send me an agent who isn't all hoofs and horns, teethed on a six-shooter.'

'Go to hell! You think *I* started that fracas?'

'Well, pardon *me* all to hell! You started the whole thing last night. Caston and Steen tried to finish it. By God! I'll say this for you: You're a ring-tailed roarer with striped wheels when it comes to gunplay. Too bad you can't play detective as well. You've finished yourself with Wells-Fargo, Shattuck.'

Boone sat down and gingerly touched his battered head. 'I didn't kill Caston. Steen opened fire. I knocked the girl out of the way. Caston knocked my cutter from my hand. Steen fired as I hit Caston. Steen's slug killed Caston. I dropped Billy with my hide-out gun.'

'Yeh?' asked Dobie quietly. 'Who saw it?'

'Jonce Maxon. Maybe the girl did, too.'

'Maxon was chased by one of the boys. He claims he saw nothing. It was too quick.'

Boone went icy-cold. 'What about Marion?'

Dobie lit a cigar. 'She was half-stunned when she hit the caliche. Says she didn't see anything, either.'

'They're both double-barreled liars! Anyone else see what happened? Or is this two-bit helltown full of liars?'

'No one has come forward as yet.'

'So?'

45

'Dowling is pinning two murder charges on you.'

'Why? I killed Steen in self-defense.'

Dobie placed his face close to the bars. 'You faced Dowling down last night and also gave him a hard time this morning in Lily Bell's beanery. Maybe you don't know the man. *No one faces him down in Willcox.* He's the hairy bear in this burg. That cold-gutted shark will see you swing for no other reason than that you had the nerve to face him down.'

'Christ!'

'You can say that again. I'll get you some jamoke. How's the *cabeza?*'

'Twice as big as it should be.' He stood up and looked through the barred window. A small group of men stood across the street looking at the jail. One of them was the big red-faced man who had been in the salon the night Dowling had faced Boone. Eli Bell. He was talking angrily. Dowling trudged down the street, ignoring Bell and the men with him.

Boone paced back and forth. The thought of Marion Maxon refusing to stand up for him hurt him a hell of a lot more than his battered head.

Dowling stood outside Boone's cell. 'I warned you,' he said. 'You didn't listen to me.'

'I didn't kill Caston.'

46

'The hell you didn't!'

'Look, Dowling. My Colt was knocked out of my hand. It was never fired. The bellygun was fired three times. Steen was hit three times. How the hell could I have shot Caston?'

Dowling's eyes narrowed. Boone was instantly sorry for what he had said.

'Steen was killed by me in self-defense.'

'You got witnesses?'

'Jonce Maxon and his daughter.'

'They claim they didn't see what happened, *hombre*.'

'Maxon is a damned liar!'

'It's your word against his, Shattuck, and you ain't in any position to have anyone listen to you.'

'I might have expected you to say that.'

Dowling's eyes were as flat and expressionless as a diamondback's. 'Don't get on the prod. Next time I'll mark you for life.' He turned and walked away.

Dobie came down the corridor. 'He's gone.' He opened the cell door and handed Boone a granite cup of jamoke. 'I heard what you said. You should have kept your mouth shut.'

'I know it now.'

'He has all the guns. Yours as well as Caston's and Steen's. I wouldn't put it past him to frame you.'

'Just because I stood up to him?'

'There's more than that, Boone,' the detective said quietly. 'He followed you out of town this morning.'

Boone looked up. 'Someone was watching me out there.'

Dobie looked back up the corridor. 'He goes out there now and then. Hell, everybody does. Personally, I doubt if the gold was ever there.'

Boone reached in his coat pocket and took out the piece of wood he had found. He handed it to Dobie. Dobie looked curiously at Boone. 'You feel all right?'

'I found that in the bottom of the woodbox out there. Notice the melted wax. There was more melted wax in the bottom of the box.'

'So?'

'Gold shipments are sealed with wax in wooden boxes. Those boxes might have been broken up out there and burned. The heat of the stove melted the wax on the wood before it was put into the stove. It dripped down.'

Dobie worked his mouth. 'Jesus! I've been out there half a dozen times and never noticed this. You might make a detective yet, Boone.'

'Yeh! With a double murder charge against me.'

Dobie scratched his jaw. 'You're not dead yet. Sheriff Mike Kelly is in Benson. He's coming down here on the east-bound tonight. This clue, slight as it is, is the first one

48

we've found that indicates that the gold might actually have been brought to Eccles' 'dobe.'

Boone emptied his cup. 'How will I get out of here?'

Dobie took the cup. 'Listen, *Brasadero*. When it comes to sheer brainwork, you leave it up to Mrs Dobie's little boy, James.'

'Keno.'

Dobie locked the cell. Boone dropped on his bunk and rolled a smoke. He lit it and watched the bluish smoke drift and waver in the air and then flow out of the small window...

The noise of the cell door being opened awoke him. Jim Dobie was looking down at him. 'Had your breakfast brought in from Lily Bell's,' he said. 'Eli brought it over.'

Eli Bell brought in a covered tray. 'Heat the jamoke, Jim,' he said.

Boone sat up. 'Damned nice of you, Eli.'

The big man sat down at the end of the bunk. 'Lily thought it up,' he said. 'Besides, I want to talk to you.'

'Shoot.'

Boone eyed the big man. He had the same amazingly big blue eyes of his buxom sister, but it was obvious he wasn't a man to be choused by Bob Dowling.

Bell lit a cigar and watched Boone eat. 'I saw Dowling last night,' he said. 'I was heading home when I saw him go into a deserted 'dobe at the edge of town. Ain't no one lived there for years. I was leavin' when I heard a shot. Bein' curious I took a look in a window. Bob was standing in the house with a smoking Colt in his hand. It wasn't his nickel-plated hogleg. Then he digs the slug outa the mattress he shot it into. He leaves the 'dobe then.'

Boone paused. 'So?'

'What did your Colt look like?'

'Sheriff's Model. Forty-four. Four-and-a-half inch barrel. Ivory grips with a Lone Star cut into them.'

Eli nodded. 'That's it!'

Boone placed the tray on the floor. 'What the hell was he up to?'

'Jim Dobie told me you killed Steen with three shots from your bellygun. Your Colt was never fired.'

'That's right.'

'Mebbe Dowling wants it to look like you *did* shoot that single-action Colt.' Bell stood up and got the tray. 'Thought you might like to know.'

'I'm obliged, Eli.'

'Forget it. I don't know you, Shattuck, but I ain't about to see Bob Dowling get away with a thing like this.' The big man left the jail.

Dobie brought in the coffee. Boone told him what Eli Bell had said. Dobie nodded. 'It figures. Mike Kelly is getting the coroner's

50

jury together. I'll take you over there after lunch.'

The long morning drifted past. About one o'clock Jim came and unlocked the cell. He handcuffed Boone with Mattatuck irons and escorted him to the schoolhouse. Six jurors sat uncomfortably on a long bench. Doc Ruffin, Assistant Coroner of Cochise County, presided. Sheriff Mike Kelly, a giant of a man with sweeping blond mustaches, came over to Boone. 'Jim told me the whole story, Shattuck,' he said.

'Did he tell you *my* side of the story?'

'Yes.'

'Dowling is out to get me.'

Kelly grinned. 'Sit tight. You ever commit a robbery in Mohave County?'

'You loco?'

Kelly grinned. 'You want to get placed in Yuma Pen, don't you?'

'Yes.' Boone figured it was all too fast for him.

'Then you held up two prospectors near Squaw Peak a year ago last February. The sixteenth, to be exact, while using the name of Jack Field. You escaped from the deputy-sheriff who was transporting you to Yuma in March of last year. You haven't been seen in Arizona until this month.'

Boone rubbed his jaw. 'You make up this tall tale?'

Kelly shook his head. 'A man by the name

of Jack Field *did* commit that robbery and was sentenced to Yuma. He *did* escape from a Mohave County law officer. But he'll never go to Yuma.'

'How so?'

'I ran him down last week near Fort Huachuca. He resisted arrest. I killed him. I haven't had time to make out a report. Instead of reporting I killed him I can say he escaped and headed for New Mexico then came back into Arizona. You follow me?'

Boone grinned. 'Yeh.'

'You play your part, sonny. Leave the rest up to Michael Francis Patrick Kelly.'

'Keno!'

The inquest began. The room was filled with curious townspeople. Matilda Bennett testified that she saw Boone walking toward Jonce Maxon's buckboard with Marion Maxon. Her husband Amos testified to the same fact. They had then gone into Corby's General Store and had heard the gunfire. Thomas Fraser, teamster, testified that he had also seen Boone and Marion walk toward the buckboard, and had also seen Casimir Caston and William Steen standing on opposite sides of the street. He had then run into the shed behind Bayliss' Blacksmith Shop. He had not seen the shooting.

Coroner Ruffin then called for witnesses Jonce and Marion Maxon. Sheriff Kelly stood up. 'A man was sent for them early this morning. They should be here within the hour.'

Ruffin scratched his beard. 'In order to speed this inquest I will call on City Marshal Robert Dowling.'

Dowling was sworn in. 'I was in the jail-house office when I heard the firing. When I reached the scene of the shooting I saw Jonce Maxon and his daughter leaving the scene in a buckboard. Boone Shattuck was standing in the middle of the street. A Colt single-action lay ten feet away from him. At his feet was a double-action Colt, altered into a bellygun.'

'Bellygun?' asked Ruffin.

'Yessir. A gun altered for a speedy draw. Barrel cut down, front of the trigger guard removed as well as the hammer spur. This is the weapon.' Dowling placed the bellygun on the table along with Boone's single-action Colt.

'Continue,' said Ruffin.

'Cass Caston was lying on his face. He had been shot through the belly and was dead. Billy Steen was lying on his back near the sidewalk. He had been shot three times through the chest.'

All eyes in the courtroom turned toward Boone. Dowling continued. 'I was forced to subdue Shattuck and then incarcerated him in the jail. I had the bodies taken to your office, Doctor Ruffin.'

Ruffin turned over the gavel to Sheriff Kelly and was sworn. His testimony, replete with medical terms, told that Caston had been killed by a slug through the abdomen. Steen had been hit three times close to the heart. Four .44/40 slugs had been removed from the bodies. Three from Steen, one from Caston. Ruffin returned to his presiding position. The door opened and Jonce Maxon came in, with Marion holding his arm. He looked deathly pale. Marion's face was drawn. She did not look at Boone.

Jonce Maxon took the stand and was sworn. 'I was waiting for my daughter Marion in my buckboard, ready to go back to my ranch,' he said in a low voice. 'This man, Shattuck, was walking with her toward me. Steen and Caston was on opposite sides of the street. My team was nervous so I wasn't watching the three men. All of a sudden this shooting starts. When I looks up I sees Caston lyin' in the street. Steen was falling. My daughter was lyin' in the street, Shattuck was in front of her with a smokin' pistol in his left hand. I got Marion into the buckboard and drove off.'

'Then you did not see who actually shot Casimer Caston?' asked Ruffin.

'No.'

'But you did see who shot Steen?'

Maxon swallowed. 'I said I seen Steen fallin' and Shattuck with a smokin' gun in his hand. I never said I seen anybody shoot at anyone else.'

Boone looked at the gangling rancher. The man was obviously lying.

Marion Maxon took the stand. 'Boone Shattuck offered to take me to my father. When we approached the buckboard we saw Cass Caston on one side of the street and Billy Steen on the other. Billy Steen stepped out and spoke to Boone Shattuck. Boone Shattuck knocked me down to protect me from the bullets. Billy Steen fired first at Boone. I saw Cass Caston run toward Boone Shattuck from behind. Mister Shattuck then had his Colt in his hand. Cass Caston struck it from his hand. Then I must have fainted.'

Boone raised his head. His eyes met those of Marion Maxon. She lowered her head.

'Did you see who shot William Steen?'

'No.'

'Did you see who shot Casimir Caston?'

'No.'

Ruffin glanced at the jury. 'That is all, Miss Maxon. City Marshal Robert Dowling to the stand.'

Dowling took the stand.

Ruffin pointed at the pistols. 'Did you examine those weapons, Mister Dowling?'

'I did. As well as the weapons carried by Steen and Caston.'

'Tell us what you found.'

Dowling stepped over to the table. 'This is

Billy Steen's gun. A .44/40 Colt single-action. It had been fired once.'

Boone's head jerked up. Maxon bit his lower lip.

'This is Cass Caston's handgun,' said Dowling. 'A Colt .41 caliber Lightning. It was loaded with five cartridges, the sixth chamber bein' empty. The gun had not been fired.'

He's right there at least, thought Boone.

Dowling glanced at Boone. 'This bellygun is .44/40 caliber. A double-action. It was loaded with five cartridges. Three of them had been fired.' Dowling picked up Boone's Sheriff's Model Colt. 'This is a .44/40 caliber Sheriff's Model Colt. I found it lying near Boone Shattuck. It had been loaded with five cartridges. *One of them had been fired.* That slug hit and killed Cass Caston.'

Ruffin glanced at the clerk. 'Do not take down that last sentence.' He looked at the jury. 'You will remember that William Steen, according to the testimony of Miss Maxon, fired *first,* at Boone Shattuck. Also that Casimir Caston, did, according to Miss Maxon's testimony, strike Boone Shattuck's pistol from his hand.'

'Are there any other witnesses to be called?' asked Ruffin.

Kelly stood up. 'Eli Bell has a statement to make.'

Bell moved up the aisle and was sworn in. 'I didn't see the shootin',' he said. 'But there is somethin' I saw that might have some bearing on this case. Last night about midnight, I was walking home when I sees City Marshal Dowling go into the old Miranda 'dobe at the edge of town. I heard a shot. I looked in through a window. Marshal Dowling was standing there with a smokin' pistol in his hand. He lays the pistol down in plain view and digs the slug out'n a mattress he had fired it into.'

Dowling rose halfway from his chair. Ruffin raised his eyebrows. 'Can you identify the weapon you saw, Mr Bell?'

Bell stood up and placed his hand on Boone's single-action Colt. 'This is it. I know it by the short barrel and the ivory grips with the star carved in 'em.'

Whispering started in the big room. Ruffin banged the gavel. 'Did you actually *see* Marshal Dowling fire the shot?'

'No.'

Dowling grinned.

Ruffin fingered his gavel and glanced at the jury. 'If there are no more witnesses the case will be summarized.'

Jim Dobie walked forward. 'I have something to say,' he said quietly. Dowling scowled at Dobie.

Jim was sworn. 'I was in the jailhouse when the first shot was fired. I looked through a cell window. Billy Steen was standing with a smoking pistol in his hand. Marion Maxon was lying on the ground. Jonce Maxon was in his buckboard. Boone Shattuck was drawing his Colt. The single-action. Cass Caston struck it from his hand. Shattuck struck Caston. Caston staggered away from him just as Billy Steen fired. The bullet struck Caston, killing him. Boone Shattuck backed away with no weapon in his hand. Steen approached him with his gun in his hand. Shattuck drew out his double-action, dropped to the ground to protect Miss Maxon and fired three times, killing Billy Steen. To my knowledge, Shattuck never fired his single-action Colt and *did not kill Casimer Caston.*'

Ruffin looked at Dobie. 'Is there anything else you have to say, Mister Dobie?'

'Yes. In shooting affairs, when the participants are arrested, their weapons are held in the jail office. City Marshal Dowling took the weapons from the scene of the shooting. This is the first time I have seen them since.'

'He's a damned liar!' yelled Dowling.

Ruffin frowned. 'Remain quiet, or you will be fined for contempt of this court!'

Boone eyed the jailor. Dobie had lied. There was no doubt in Boone's mind about that.

The jury left the schoolroom. In twenty minutes they returned. Doc Ruffin read the verdict. 'Territory of Arizona, County of Cochise. An inquisition, holden in the county of Cochise, territory of Arizona, on the 15th

58

day of May, A.D. 1889, before me, Jonas Ruffin, Assistant Coroner of Cochise County, Territory of Arizona, upon the bodies of William Steen and Casimer Caston, by the persons whose names are hereto subscribed. The said jurors upon their oaths, from the evidence do say that the said Casimer Caston was accidentally killed by a bullet wound from a pistol fired by William Steen, since deceased, on the 13th day of May, 1889, in the county of Cochise, Territory of Arizona. That the said William Steen came to his death by three bullet wounds from a pistol fired by Boone Shattuck in self-defense, on the 13th day of May, 1889, in the county of Cochise, Territory of Arizona.'

Dowling got to his feet. 'Bell,' he said. 'You'll pay for this!'

Sheriff Mike Kelly came close to the two big men. 'Dowling, I've heard about your foul record hereabouts. If the people of Willcox have any pride they'll kick you out of that job of yours!'

'Go to hell!' said Dowling.

Jim Dobie came toward them. Dowling whirled. 'Here's another damned liar!' he roared. Suddenly, as though reason had departed, he slapped his hand down for a draw. Boone jumped from his chair. He gripped the big marshal by the arm and whirled him about. His wrists were still encircled with the heavy Mattatuck irons. He swung both arms to the side and smashed his clasped hands against Dowling's heavy jaw. The marshal grunted and staggered back. Blood streamed from his mouth. He hit Dowling again. The marshal threw up his arms and turned to run. Boone smashed his hands against the back of Dowling's head. Dowling did not see the window in front of him. He smashed through the glass, hanging on the sill. Glass tinkled down.

Boone stepped back, looking at the unconscious marshal. Dobie pulled him back through the window. His face was slashed to ribbons. 'Jesus,' Jim said.

Sheriff Kelly thrust a long arm in between Boone and Dobie as the jailor held out the key to unlock the irons. 'This man is wanted for robbery in Mohave County. Under the alias of Jack Field he robbed two men near Squaw Mountain last year. He escaped from a deputy-sheriff who was escorting him to Yuma Penitentiary last year.'

'Well I'll be double-damned!' said Eli Bell.

Dobie handed the key to Sheriff Kelly. 'He's your prisoner, Mike.'

The last thing Boone saw as Kelly walked him back toward the calabozo was Marion Maxon, standing beside her father, just outside the schoolhouse.

Her eyes told the story of her thoughts.

CHAPTER SIX

A cold wind whispered over Prison Hill and moaned softly through the long cell corridor. Boone shivered in the thin-striped coat and pants he had been issued, as he trudged between two burly guards down the dimly lit corridor. His scalp itched from the close shave in the prison barber shop. The harsh leather of the square-toed prison shoes irked feet that had worn nothing but boots.

The screws stopped before a barred cell door and unlocked the heavy padlock set through a thick hasp three feet from the edge of the narrow door. He removed the padlock, lifted the hasp and threw his weight against the metal bar which actuated both the inner and outer doors of the cell. They creaked open. The second screw shoved Boone forward. 'In!'

Boone walked into the gloomy cell. Both doors creaked shut behind him.

'Fresh fish,' a hoarse voice said from a lower bunk.

A man giggled from an upper bunk. Boone stood in a narrow cell between the tiered metal bunks, three on a side, eight feet high. He stumbled over a thick metal ring set into the cell floor.

'Any room?' asked Boone.

The man in the lower bunk laughed. 'Any room in Yuma! Hawww!'

'Take the top or middle bunk to your right,' a shadow said from the lower left bunk. He chuckled. 'We're lucky, us short-timers. Only got three of us in here ... four, counting you.'

Boone threw his mattress cover and blanket into the middle bunk. There was barely enough room for an average sized man to fit into the bunk.

A squat man thrust thick legs over the side of the right hand lower bunk. 'The name is Concho Bates,' he said. 'Two years for armed robbery.' He thrust out a ham of a hand.

Boone gripped it. 'Boone Shattuck. One year for armed robbery. Six months for escaping before they landed me here.'

Bates jerked his head. 'The skinny man behind you is Benny Hatch. Two years for knifing a gambler at Gila Bend.'

Benny giggled.

'Thalus Hastings,' the man in the left hand lower bunk said. 'A year for attempted robbery.' His voice seemed cultured.

Boone looked toward the back of the cell. It was blocked by a cross hatching of thick double bars. Beyond the bars was another cell, exactly like the one he was in. 'Shut up in there!' a man yelled. 'We wanta sleep!'

'Go to hell, Dixie!' said Concho.

62

'I'll kick the crap outa you tomorrow!' said Dixie.

Concho laughed deep in his throat. 'Yuh tried it two months ago. Remember what happened?'

'Go to hell!' said Dixie.

Boone made up his bunk and rolled into it. There was a rank smell in the cell; the mingled odors of sweat, urine, stale bedding and unwashed feet.

Concho said, 'Yuh got any smokin' material?'

'They cleaned me.'

'Damned screws won't even let a man have a smoke at night.'

'No smokin' here,' said Benny Hatch. He giggled. 'Anyways, *I* don't smoke.'

'Clean livin' bastard,' grunted Concho. 'Don't smoke or drink. But don't turn your back on him when he's got a knife in his dirty hand.'

Boone wriggled about. The mattress was packed and lumpy.

Thalus Hastings laughed. 'It's not much worse than sleeping on the ground, Shattuck.'

'It's the stink yuh got to get used to,' said Concho.

Boone covered himself with his blanket. 'I doubt if I will.'

'You're from Texas,' Hastings said.

Boone glanced down at the shadowy face,

63

thin and ascetic in the dim light. 'Yes.'

'I'm from Kentucky. Lived in Texas for a time.'

'Yeh,' said Concho. 'They had him in Huntsville for forgery.'

'Nice place Texas,' said Hastings.

Concho yawned. 'I'm from Missouri. Show me.'

Benny giggled. 'You ain't seen Old Chi,' he said.

'Old Chi?' asked Boone.

'Chicago. Real booming town after they rebuilt it. Nice fillies there.' Benny giggled. 'Once I get out of this hellhole I'm headin' for Frisco. They say it's like Old Chi.'

'I'll give you a week there,' said Hastings dryly. 'Then you'll end up in the pokey again.'

'Shut up in there!' yelled Dixie.

'Come and make us,' jeered Concho. 'You damned long-legged rebel.'

Silence answered him.

Concho leaned out of his bunk and looked up at Boone. 'Dixie is the rooster in that cell. I'm the hairy bear in this one. Yuh clean up the cell this next month and me and the boys will go easy on yuh.'

'Fair enough,' said Boone.

'Some of the cells have a kangaroo court on fresh fish. Dixie give a new man a going over last week because he thought he was tough. Ended up in the infirmary. He's a good boy now. We'll go easy on you, Boone.'

Boone grinned in the semi-darkness.

Concho eyed him. 'Hard case, eh?'

'Hard enough.'

'Shut up,' said Thalus Hastings. 'Never let it be said that Cell Two didn't consider a man's feelings his first night away from home.'

'Jeeeesus!' said Concho.

Benny giggled.

'How's the chuck?' asked Boone.

'Slop,' said Concho.

'Anything to do here?'

Thalus laughed. 'Mattress shop. Tailor shop. Laundry. Library. Blacksmith. Bakery. Messhall. Supply shop. Workshops. What can you do?'

'Punch cows. Pack mules. Scout. Break horses.'

'Most of the plushy jobs are taken by old-timers. Probably end up in the laundry,' said Hastings.

'Ain't bad in the winter,' said Concho. 'Sheer hell in the summer.'

The cold wind swept through the cells. Boone shivered.

Concho coughed. 'Like I said: I'm the hairy bear in here, Shattuck. Don't never forget it.'

Benny giggled. 'Yeh, when Bass Eccles ain't in here, you are.'

Boone's eyes snapped open.

'Bass ain't so much,' growled Concho.

65

'You sure walk quiet when he *is* here,' said Benny.

'I'll break your waggin' jaw!' blustered Concho.

'Who's Bass Eccles?' asked Boone.

Thalus leaned out of his bunk. 'Short-termer. Robber. Used to have your bunk.'

'Where is he now?'

'The Snake Den,' said Concho. He laughed. 'Eccles got lippy with Cap Ingalls, the warden. Ingalls had him thrown into the Snake Den until his time is up.'

'What's the Snake Den?'

'Cell for incorrigibles,' said Thalus. 'Hewn out of solid granite. Right across from the cell block entrance. A bitch of a place.'

'Just right for Eccles,' said Concho.

Boots slapped on the concrete of the corridor. A shadowy figure stood outside the outer door. Concho waited until the guard walked away. 'Bastard,' he said.

Boone closed his eyes. Yuma Pen was fourteen years old. Seven prisoners had been the first contingent. Additional prisoners had built the cell blocks and prison buildings. Ten acres atop a granite bluff that pushed its way into the yellow waters of the Colorado. Now the prison held over three hundred, some of them from states and territories other than Arizona.

In two days, Kelly had taken Boone from Willcox, manacled and under guard. They had left the train at the Yuma station and Boone had been stripped of his clothing, ordered to bathe, and had his head shaved by a lifer. Captain Ingalls had given him advice on his conduct and then he had been locked in this filthy, cold cell.

If Eccles got word that Boone was an undercover man, Boone would never leave Yuma unless he was sewed into his blanket and buried on the slope near the river.

The guards' whistles blew just after dawn. Boone dropped from his bunk and looked about the white-plastered cell. The ceiling was arched and smoothly plastered. Some past inmate had scored the word, Libertad, in the smooth plaster. 'Liberty,' he translated.

Thalus Hastings yawned from his bunk. 'Jesus Diaz cut that in there six months ago.'

Concho spat on the floor. 'Yeh. The screws figgered he was tryin' to cut through. He got a month in the Snake Den. Never come out. Went loco. They stuck him in the insane cell. I helped bury the poor bastard.'

'Wouldn't have done him any good trying to get through there,' said Hastings. 'You see those bars between us and the next cell? Well, those bars are on each side of us and all the way up over the top. Like a cage covered with plaster. Besides, Jesus just wanted to lie in his bunk and look at the word he had inscribed.'

He laughed harshly. *'Liberty, indeed!'*

Thalus Hastings was about forty-five, thin and intelligent looking. His prison garb hung loosely on his tall spare figure.

Benny Hatch was a little man, like a weasel, with washed-out eyes and a hooked nose that seemed to tremble. Concho stood up and pulled back his striped coat revealing a barrel chest covered thickly with stiff black hair. His dark eyes studied Boone. 'Yuh clean up good, yuh hear?'

Boone nodded. Concho balled a big fist. 'I don't want no bitchin' from the screws.' He clamped a big hand about Boone's left wrist. Boone eyed the hand. 'Take it away,' he said quietly. The man was as strong as an ox. Concho exerted more pressure. 'Sure, sure,' he growled. He stepped back, a naked challenge in his small dark eyes.

Boone dropped to the floor and began cleaning up the cell with a worn broom. 'Sweep in the corners!' ordered Concho.

The double doors swung open and they filed out into the corridor. Up and down the rows of cells Boone heard the clank of chains. 'Some of the boys are chained to that big ring you saw in the cell floor,' said Hastings. 'We're short-termers so they don't bother to chain us.'

'Any breaks here?' said Boone.

Thalus shrugged. 'Now and then. Work parties mostly. A year ago three of them

68

tried it. The watchtower is set up over the big cistern. They have a Gatling up there. Two of the boys were killed before they got two hundred yards. The last of them made the river and drowned.'

Mess was doughy mush, strong black coffee and bristly sowbelly. The men ate noisily. There was no talking; no sound other than the clatter of utensils and the shuffling of feet on the gritty floor. A screw banged on a table with his truncheon. 'All new inmates will fall in outside the door for an inspection tour.' He grinned. 'Welcome to Yuma Pen.'

Boone shuffled out with a string of bowed men.

'We use the messhall for a chapel,' said the leading guard. 'Some of you bastards could use a little Bible learning.' He led them past the blacksmith and bakery and then to the supply building overlooking the town. Boone looked across Yuma. There was a small park between Prison Hill and the S.P. tracks. Slabsided houses stood starkly out on bare ground on a ridge beyond the tracks. 'Hell of a place,' murmured a man behind him.

They skirted the main cell block past the building where the solitary cells were. The guard stopped and pointed to the end of a granite hill that stood up at the end of the ten acre prison area. 'Them's the women's cells overlookin' the town,' he said with a grin. 'Don't get any ideas of consortin' with

69

the female prisoners.' He walked along a row of doorways cut into the naked granite. 'That's the insane cell there. Take a look,' he invited. Boone looked into a roughly hewn cell. It was just big enough for a man. Even the low bunk had been hewn from the stone.

'Cell One is for visitin',' said the guard. 'Not that you scum can expect any visitors. Two and Three are for the violently insane. Some of you will probably end up there.'

'Nice hombre,' said a convict.

'Shut up!' roared a guard.

'Cell Four is the Mattress Shop,' said the guide. 'We train the boys in there to make them as uncomfortable as possible.'

The leading guard stopped at a narrow door. 'This is Cell Five. The Snake Den. This is for incorrigables! You get out of line, you go in there and about one outa every ten goes nuts in there. Then we shift him down to the Insane Cell. There ain't no way outa the Snake Den except through two barred doors. Solid granite all around and over your head. Remember that!'

The guard led them through a gateway set in a thick wall. 'That row of cells is extra, for hard cases.' He paused and pointed up. 'You see them towers? Guards up there with rifles. Dead shots, every one of 'em.' He led the way back through the gateway and along the workshops to the toilets set near a squat,

70

low-roofed tower built above a stone cistern. 'Yuh see that Gatling? It covers every inch of open ground. Don't get any ideas on makin' breaks here.' He pointed down a slope to a fenced enclosure. 'Cemetery.' The morning sun cast faint shadows behind the redwood headboards.

The guard turned to his two mates. 'Take 'em back to their cells.' He stalked off.

Boone eyed the rock walls enclosing the ten acre prison tract. Men lounged about the prison yard. One of the guards spoke over his shoulder. 'You can stay in the prison yard from seven A.M. until five P.M. unless you got work to do. No fighting. No groups.'

Boone wandered over to where Thalus Hastings sat with his back to the wall. Concho Bates leaned beside him. Benny Hatch was idly tossing a stone up and down. 'Yuh get the Grand Tour?' asked Concho with a grin.

Boone nodded.

'There isn't a damned thing to do unless they assign you to one of the shops,' said Thalus. 'I work in the library. Spend the day reading. Makes the time go.'

'Wish that I could read,' said Benny.

'Offered to teach you,' said Thalus dryly.

Concho spat. 'Hellsfire! Readin'! Why don't they let us have some cards?'

'Bad for the morals,' said Thalus.

A man squatted not far from them patiently

71

knitting a bedspread. His gnarled fingers moved slowly.

'Jesse Bardolph,' said Thalus. 'A lifer. Makes the best bedcovers I ever saw. Sells them to visitors. Damned if I know what he does with the money though.'

Boone sat down and took off his left shoe. His heel was rubbing raw. A man rounded the corner, an angry look on his lean face. 'Here comes Dixie Yates,' said Benny.

Concho balled big hairy fists and looked at him. 'I hope he tries to get proddy,' he said.

'He's looking for Shattuck,' Thalus said.

The tall man eyed Boone. Two other men watched the trio next to the wall as though anticipating something. Yates sauntered over. 'Who was doin' all the jawin' last night?' he asked in a slow drawl.

'All of us was,' said Concho. 'Why?'

Yates' icy eyes studied Boone. 'I got no bone to pick with you, Bates,' he said. 'It's this new fish.'

Boone looked up. 'I'm sorry,' he said.

'He's sorry,' Yates said over his shoulder. The two watching men laughed. The southerner looked at Boone's unshod foot. 'Shoe pinchin'?' he asked.

Boone nodded.

'Ain't you got no manners?'

'I don't follow you, Yates.'

Yates yawned. 'Your feet stink. Smelled 'em

72

plum over in our cell. The boys asked me to tell yuh to keep 'em clean.'

Men began to gather. One of them stood near the corner of the cell block, watching for a guard.

Boone pulled on his shoe. 'Surprising you could smell me over your stink, Yates.'

Yates went red. 'You lookin' for trouble?'

Boone stood up. 'No. But I don't aim to crawfish.'

'Yuh forgot to tie your shoe,' Yates said.

Boone looked down. Yates stepped in. His long right arm lashed out. The hard fist knocked Boone back against the wall. Yates stepped in close and drove in a hard one-two that sent Boone down.

Yates blew on his fists and looked back at the watcher. 'Any screws around, Jimmy?' he called.

'Nary a one, Dixie.'

Boone wiped the blood from his mouth as he got up. Yates danced about easily, shadow boxing. 'Had enough?' he asked.

Boone nodded. Concho growled in his throat.

Yates looked back over his shoulder. 'He's yella,' he said.

Boone uncorked a driving left which clipped Yates' lean jaw, a right jab which staggered him. His left sank to the wrist in the lean gut of the southerner. His right came up short and hard, connecting solidly with Yates'

73

chin. Yates went down hard. He bounced to his feet and rushed Boone, throwing punishing blows. Boone danced aside and Yates drove a wild blow against the cell block behind Boone. Yates screamed.

'Screw comin',' yelled Jimmy.

Yates thrust his bleeding hands into his pants' pocket and leaned back against the wall. Boone squatted beside Hastings. The guard rounded the corner. 'Spread out, you bastards!' He stopped short and looked at Boone. 'Your mouth is bleeding.'

'Yeh.'

'How'd you do it?' The guard looked at Yates.

Boone grinned. 'Fell up a wall.'

The guard rubbed his thick jaw. 'I'll remember you. What's your name?'

'Boone Shattuck.'

'The man who killed those two men down in Willcox a week ago?'

All eyes turned toward Boone. Boone nodded.

'Hard case, eh?'

Boone looked at him.

'Well, I catch any of you fools fighting and you'll end up in the Snake Den.' The guard walked away.

Concho eyed Boone. 'Thought you said you was in for robbery?'

'I am.'

Concho jerked his head in the direction

74

where the guard had gone. 'What'd he mean?'

'I killed *one* man down in Willcox. He killed his *amigo* with a wild shot. The sheriff picked me up on an old robbery charge.'

Yates paled a little, licked his abraded hand. 'I ain't done with you,' he said.

Benny grinned. 'He wasn't done with you, neither.'

The tall southerner walked away.

'You handled him right nice,' Concho said.

Hastings nodded. 'Watch him, Shattuck. He's mean.'

Boone nodded. The words of the guard came back to him. *I catch any of you bastards fighting and you'll end up in the Snake Den.*

Concho watched Boone through veiled eyes. 'I know Willcox,' he said. 'Who was it you knocked off there?'

'Billy Steen. Cass Caston was the other *hombre*.'

'Billy Steen? I knew him down to Bisbee. He had bobcat bristles on his belly.'

'He hasn't anymore.'

'How'd yuh do it?' asked Benny eagerly.

'Gun hassle. Billy drew and missed. Killed Caston. I dropped Steen.'

'Steen was fast with a six-gun,' said Concho. 'Near as fast as Bass Eccles. They was *amigos* once.'

Boone looked out across the prison yard to

75

the distant hazy Gilas. Suddenly a wild unreasoning surge swept over him. He wanted to yell out, race for the wall and scale it, and bury himself in the sandy brushy wastes to the east.

'Don't try it,' advised Thalus softly.

Boone looked at him.

'It comes over all of us the first week or so in here. Take it easy, Boone.'

Boone wiped his face. 'It's gettin' warm,' he said.

Concho nodded. 'It'll get warmer. Hell of a place. Freeze in winter. Roast in summer. I've heard it said the mercury dries up in August around here.'

'Everything dries up,' said Thalus. 'Wagons. Men. Chickens. All the juices dry up. People creak when they walk. Mules bray only at night. The carcasses of cattle dry inside their hides and rattle like bones. Snakes find it hard to bend. Horned frogs die of apoplexy.'

'Hell!' said Benny. 'Listen to him!'

Concho grinned. 'Heard tell of a soldier from Fort Yuma, across the river, who died and went to hell one blasting summer day. That night his ghost comes back and asks the quartermaster to re-issue his blankets. He couldn't stand the drop in temperature down there! Hawww!'

Thalus rolled his eyes upwards. 'Makes me want to try for Mexico. Only twenty-six miles south of here.'

'You'd never make it,' said Benny.

Concho shook his head. 'They got Yuma and special trackers around here. Johnny the Dip got away once with Jesse Ebbetts. They got as far as Martinez Well, north-east of here. Johnny sees Yuma trackers. He breaks for the brush. Jessie surrenders. The Yumas didn't bother to haul Jesse back. Brung in his head in a sack. They got fifty dollars. Johnny the Dip comes back on his own. Went loco, thinkin' about Jesse. They buried him six months later.'

At noon mess Boone felt Dixie Yates' eyes on him. At supper the lanky southerner dropped a pot of coffee behind Boone and burned his back with the hot liquid. On the way back to the cells Thalus Hastings spoke. 'He'll ride you until you fight again. This time he'll try to maim you.'

That night Boone lay in his bunk, the snores of the other men driving sleep from him. He thought of Marion Maxon. If Dobie hadn't perjured himself Boone might have been sent to Yuma for life, if they hadn't strung him up instead. Maybe she had been protecting her weak father. He covered his face with his hands. Marion Maxon seemed to haunt him.

To her he was nothing but a number in the hellhole on Prison Hill.

CHAPTER SEVEN

A week dragged by. The heat began to get hellish. Summer was early. Sweat soaked the rough striped suits and then dried. There was a constant odor of urine, sweat and un-washed bodies about the bare cells; a miasma which clung in the cell block and sickened Boone. He thought often of the days along the Brazos. At night he could hear the wild screaming of an inmate confined in one of the stone cubicles for the insane and then the yelling of the guards as they clubbed the poor wretch into unconsciousness.

Boone's solid frame began to thin out. He thought of *chili, olla podrida, enchiladas* and *panoches* until he felt his mouth fill with water. The prison fare was coarse, prepared by convict cooks. The very smell of the mess-hall was enough to turn a man's gut.

Boone was put to work in the laundry. The steaming tubs filled the air with fog. Sweat rolled from his body and dripped into the tubs with the soapy water. He looked over the stone walls at the distant mountains and a wild urge to break free would sweep over him, almost overpowering in its intensity, but Thalus Hastings always seemed to know when it was at its worst, and his quiet voice drove away the mad desire to break free.

The sun was beating down and the guard in charge of the laundry let them off an hour early. Boone went to the toilets to find Thalus who had taken his turn there as orderly. The lean man wasn't there but Dixie Yates was, leaning against the wall with two of his mates. Yates grinned. 'Watch the door, Sam. Keep an eye outa the window, Jimmy.'

Boone turned toward the door. Sam leaned against it, grinning at him. Yates swaggered up to Boone. 'Well,' he said thinly, 'you ready to take it up again?'

Boone wiped his hands on his coat. 'You want the screws to come in?'

'You bastard,' Yates said. 'I'da broke you in half if that screw hadn't horned in.' He rushed Boone and drove in a stinging right. Boone covered up, blocking a hard left, and fell back. Yates circled slowly, like a copperhead ready to strike. 'Yuh had an advantage the first time,' he said. 'Full of good chuck from outside. Yuma thinned you down to the right size.'

Yates closed in. Boone straightened him with a left and brought over a whistling right which drove the tall man against the wall, stepped in and smashed Yates' head back against the wall. Yates sagged.

'Go get him, Dixie!' said the big man at

the door.

Yates drove in at Boone. Boone stopped him with jabs and hooked in a vicious right which sent Dixie reeling across the room. 'Come on, Dixie!' implored Jimmy.

'Watch that damned window!' said Yates out of his smashed mouth.

Yates suddenly rushed in, stepped on Boone's right foot and hit him with both fists to the face. Boone crashed to the floor and rolled away from Yates' smashing feet. He got to his knees and went down again from a kick to the ribs. Yates stood over him, waiting for him to get up. When he didn't, Yates started to lift him by the hair.

Boone pulled back and smashed a blow to the tall man's groin. As Yates bent forward Boone drove up with his head and hit Yates square in the face. Blood spattered down on Boone. He jumped away. Yates yelled, pawing at his face with reddened hands. Boone hit him in the gut and drove him back against the wall. Sam left his post and rushed in. Boone whirled, caught the burly man with a right and then hit Yates with a vicious uppercut. Yates went down, striking his neck on the edge of a toilet.

'Guards!' yelled Jimmy. 'Shattuck is fightin' again!'

Sam hit Boone with a short left. Boone hung on to the big man and they reeled about the stinking room. Sam fell over Yates'

80

legs with Boone on top. He gripped Sam by the collar and battered his head against the hard floor.

'He's killin' my pals!' yelled Jimmy.

Boone was jerked back. Something hit hard just over his left ear. He went down into a whirling pit of blackness and knew no more...

Something was poking into Boone's pocket. He groaned. He was roughly rolled over. 'Clean as a coot,' a dry voice said in disgust.

Boone opened his eyes. His face was flat against a hard stone floor. He gently touched over his left ear. Blood coated the side of his head.

'It ain't busted,' the voice said. 'Yuh got a thick head, brother, in more ways than one.'

Boone rolled over and sat up. A chain clanked. He moved his left leg. The chain clanked again. A stub of a candle guttered from a niche in the rough-hewn stone wall. A tall, stoop-shouldered man sat with his back against the wall, eyeing Boone. 'You sure raised hell in the craphouse,' he said.

Boone winced as he moved his head. 'Where the hell am I?'

The tall man laughed. 'In the Snake Den. By God! You musta had a helluva fight. The screw tells me Dixie Yates has a cracked skull and Sam Penner ain't much better off. You're a good man with your fists, Shattuck,

81

even if yuh ain't very bright.'

Boone shook his head. 'I feel like they threw me off Prison Hill.'

'Hawww! They sure heaved you in here.'

The yellow candlelight showed on the man's bald head. The man grinned lop-sidedly. 'I'm Bass Eccles. Mebbe yuh heard of me?'

Boone nodded.

Eccles chuckled. The light showed his piercing black eyes. 'Seems like everybody knows about old Bass Eccles.'

Boone nodded. He looked about the notorious cell. It was about fifteen feet square and ten feet high, hewn out of solid rock, the rough walls blackened by smoke and covered with cobwebs. His left ankle was ringed and chained to a large iron ring set into the rock floor. Over his head was a square hole through which he could see the graying sky through many feet of solid granite.

There was a furtive movement in a dark corner. 'Who's that?' asked Boone.

Eccles grinned. 'Pedro Loco.' He stood up with a clank of chains and took the candle from the niche. He held it toward the corner. A small man was hunched there, wrapped in a ragged blanket, his wizened face staring without concentration at Boone.

'Who is he?' asked Boone. The mindless stare made his skin crawl.

Eccles shoved the little man with his foot.

'My cellmate until you come in. Say hello, Pedro.'

Pedro did not move.

Boone looked at Eccles. 'He out of his mind?'

'Yeh. Plumb loco.'

Suddenly the little man began to scream thinly, his shrill voice rising higher and higher. He pointed a dirty finger at Boone. 'You're dead!' he said in swift Spanish. 'Go away! You're dead! Jesus! Mary! Send him away! Covered with blood!'

'Shut up, Pedro,' Eccles said.

The Mexican screamed. Eccles gripped the demented man by the neck and smashed a fist against the little man's jaw, driving his head back against the stone wall. Pedro's shrill, haunting voice cut off short. He slid to the floor. Eccles wiped his hands on his trousers. 'Pedro sees things,' he said. 'I gotta smash him now and then. Only way I get any sleep around here.'

Boone looked down at the unconscious man. Blood ran from his slack mouth. Eccles placed the candle back in the niche. 'Pedro useta eat peyote. He got on a peyote jag and thought he was an executioner or somethin'. Gets his machete and lops the heads off'n his wife, brother-in-law and a cousin. Now and agin he sees 'em starin' at him from the shadows. Three bloody heads in a row. Goes off his *cabeza*.' Eccles grinned. 'Takes a good

83

man to keep from goin' that in here.'

Boone sat down with his back against the wall. 'How do you stand it?'

'Me?' Eccles grinned slyly. 'I got dreams, brother. Dreams. Things I aim to do onct I get outa here.'

'For instance?'

Eccles sat down, leaning back against the wall. 'Get me a *hacienda* down in Mexico. Maybe Guatemala or Nicaragua. Get me a nice brown-skinned filly, slender in the pasterns and smooth in the flank. Mebbe about sixteen years old. Be a real *don, amigo, a real don.*'

Boone grinned. 'Don't hurt to dream. Takes *dinero* for things like that. You got it?'

Eccles' eyes veiled. 'I didn't say so.'

'You aim to make a killin' when you get out?'

'Yeh. That's it. A killin'.'

Boone sighed. 'I tried it. Held up two prospectors near Squaw Mountain. Damned near got away with six thousand in gold.'

'Peanuts.'

Boone grinned. 'Maybe you've got a *morral* in here loaded with pesos? Where is it hidden?'

'Where is *what* hidden?' There was cold menace in Eccles' tone.

Boone yawned. 'All the gold you'll need for that *hacienda.*'

'I didn't say I had anything hidden.'

'No.'

Pedro groaned. Eccles aimed a boot and kicked hard against his jaw. Pedro went out again. Eccles glanced at Boone. 'Where you from?'

'Texas.'

'Then you shoulda been put in Huntsville.'

'Squaw Mountain is in Arizona, *amigo*. In the Cerbats.'

'You mean Squaw Peak.'

'Same thing.'

'Yeh. The screw said something about a killin' in Willcox.' The dark veiled eyes studied Boone.

Boone nodded. 'Had a fallin' out with two *hombres*. They went on the prod for me. We had it out.'

'Real hard case, eh?' Eccles eased the ring about his skinny ankle. 'Who was the men you tangled with?'

'Names of Billy Steen and Cass Caston.'

'Yeh.'

'You know them?'

'Useta. I useta be city marshal there.'

'You're joshin'!'

'Hell no! Useta be deputy-sheriff down in Cochise County, too. Everybody down there knows Bass Eccles. Didn't you ever hear of me?'

'Sounds familiar.'

'Yeh.' Eccles leaned back against the wall.

'I only got a couple weeks to go in here.'

'Then back to Cell Two?'

Eccles slowly shook his bald head. 'No.'

'You aimin' to make a break?'

'I ain't sayin'.' He eyed Boone. 'You must be rough as a cob. Kill Billy Steen, a good man with a hogleg. Beat up Dixie Yates and his *amigo,* Sam. Rough as a cob.'

Boone waved a dirty hand.

Eccles nodded. 'How long you got to go?'

'Year and a half. Year for armed robbery. Six months for breakin' away from the guard takin' me here. If I'da had any sense I would have got over into Sonora. Instead I circle down through Chihuahua, up into El Paso, then back into Arizona.'

'Why?'

'Figured I'd head for California. I shoulda had enough sense to stay outa trouble. Instead I tangle with Steen and Caston. I was freed on self-defense and then Sheriff Kelly recognizes me from a Wanted poster.'

'Mike Kelly is no fool.'

Boone nodded.

'Too bad. How's Willcox?'

'Just the same.'

'Bob Dowling still marshal?'

Boone grinned. 'He was. Perjured himself and lost his job. That's one good thing I did back there anyway.'

'Yuh mean he perjured himself in a case against you?'

86

'Keno.'

'Why?'

'I stood up to him. He didn't like it.'

'Sounds like Bob, all right.'

Boone looked up at the chimney hole. 'Can a man fit in that?'

'Hell no! If you're aimin' to escape, play it smart, and wait until yuh get outa this hole. Fact is, yuh can't get outa here. Take it easy and wait until yuh get out.'

'What then?'

'You figure it out. Now shut up. I want some shuteye.'

Eccles eased down to the floor and in a few minutes was snoring. Boone eyed the bald-headed outlaw. It would be so damned easy to strangle him while he slept. Pedro Loco groaned in his sleep. Boone closed his eyes. His head throbbed. The place stank. In a hole inside a granite hill with a cold-blooded outlaw and a demented mass murderer.

'Hell,' he said softly. 'What a price to pay.'

Boone opened his eyes to stare in almost Stygian darkness. He sat bolt upright, the cold sweat of fear dewing his body. A chain clanked. There was a savage grunt. 'Shattuck!! Shattuck!' The frenzied cry was cut short. Bass Eccles. Boone stretched a hand in the darkness.

'Shattuck! For God's … sake … he's strangling … me … with his … chain!'

Boone reached out and felt the thin form of the demented Mexican. Teeth gnawed at his right forearm. He set himself and struck hard. Pedro Loco gasped. The chain clanked. Boone ran his hands down the maniac's thin arms and gripped the tightly clenched hands. They were holding a leg chain twisted tightly about Eccles' neck. Boone pried at the unseen fingers. The little Mexican had the power of a much bigger man. Eccles gasped as the chain loosened. Boone went down over the sprawled outlaw, pulling Pedro with him. The rank stench of the maniac flooded his nostrils. A knee came up in his groin. A chain lashed across Boone's face starting a flood of tears. Blood ran from his nose.

Boone rolled atop the struggling madman and banged the head down on the stone floor. Pedro threw him off. Over and over they went, battling in the darkness until Boone's leg chain drew taut. He kneed his opponent in the groin and battered at the unseen face. The Mexican screamed. Eccles was silent in the darkness.

Yellow lantern light flooded the narrow entranceway. 'What the hell is going on?' yelled a screw.

'Loco is out of his mind!' gasped Boone. He hit the Mexican in the gut, hammered at the thin face.

The door creaked open and the lantern flooded the Snake Den. Boone drove in a jolting right that put Pedro Loco into the long sleep. Boone stood up and wiped the blood from his face. The screw unlocked Pedro Loco's chain and dragged the unconscious man through the entranceway. Boone felt for the candle. He lit it and leaned his head against the stone wall. Fear and exertion soaked his shaking body with cold sweat. Suddenly he looked up. What had happened to Bass Eccles?

Eccles crouched in a corner with his dirty hands covering his lean face.

'Eccles,' said Boone.

The outlaw did not move.

'Eccles!'

Eccles lowered his hands and looked at Boone with eyes of naked fear. His body shook. He slowly reached up and touched his abraded neck. Boone had seen men gripped by green slavering fear before, but Eccles' terror was branded on his soul, making him appear inhuman.

Boone picked up the water olla and threw some on Eccles. Eccles threw himself on the floor and shook in a paroxysm of fear. Broken sobs emanated from the terror-stricken man.

Boone heard the clanging of the cell door farther down the row as the guard threw Pedro Loco into the insane cell. Boone touched his damaged face and wiped the blood from his nose. He watched the outlaw and a stark truth seemed to stalk through the dingy stone room. Bass Eccles had a yellow streak as wide as his streak of assumed bravado. Boone filed it away in his mind. It might eventually destroy Bass Eccles.

'Rise and shine,' a voice said. 'Chuck.'

Boone opened his eyes and rolled over. His face was swollen. Bass Eccles squatted near the door looking with disgust at the bowls of food in front of him. The guard eyed Boone. 'How do you feel,' he asked.

'Rough.'

'Pedro Loco has been raving all night. The doc says he ain't got long to live.'

Eccles spat. 'Hope the bastard dies. This chuck is hog slop.'

'Maybe you'd like a steak?' asked the guard.

'Yeh. I'll be eating steaks, Martin, when you're still eatin' this prison swill.' Quite different from the terror-stricken man who had been groveling on the floor a few hours before.

Boone eyed the outlaw. Eccles yawned. 'Well, Martin, get outa here and let us eat. We like privacy.'

The guard grunted and left.

'How do you feel?' asked Eccles. He did not look at Boone.

'Lousy.'

'Yeh. It *was* rough.' Eccles swallowed noisily. 'I won't forget it, Shattuck.'

'It was nothing.'

Eccles touched his bruised throat. 'Yeh. Nothin'.' Boone finished his meal and drank the rank coffee. Eccles handed him the makings. Boone stared at the tobacco. 'Where'd you get it?'

Eccles waved a hand. 'I got connections.'

'I guess you have.' Boone rolled a smoke and lit up. He watched the bluish smoke drift up through the chimney hole. 'Tastes good.'

'Mexican crap. I'll buy yuh a wad of real Virginny smokin' tobacco onct we get out.'

Boone eyed the lean man. He had said *we*.

'I ain't got long to go,' Eccles said.

'Wish I could say that.'

'Yuh don't have to stay in here.'

Boone clanked his leg chain. 'What do I do? Ask to get out?'

'Don't get funny.'

Boone smoked slowly and then rolled another cigarette. 'Where you headin' when you get out?'

The dark eyes glanced at Boone. 'I told yuh.'

Boone grinned. 'Yeh. A hacienda down in Nicaragua you said. With a sixteen year old gal. I mean, where are you really headin'?'

'I told yuh!'

'You must think I'm simple as a kit beaver.'

Eccles leaned back against the wall. 'Can you swim?'

91

'Learned how in the Brazos.'

'I mean *good?*'

'Better than most cowpokes.' Eccles nodded.

'Why?'

Eccles' dark eyes were half-closed. 'I don't swim worth a damn.'

'I'd teach you if we weren't in this hole.'

'Yuh don't have to teach me. Just give me a hand.'

Boone scratched his jaw. 'Keep talkin'.'

Eccles got up and walked to the door dragging his chain. He peered out and then came back. 'Listen! I'm gettin' out. I'll need help. Any man can down Billy Steen and lick Dixie Yates, not to mention what you done for me last night, is my man.'

Boone inspected his smoke. 'You forgot something. I've got eighteen months to go.'

'Would you make a break if you had the chance?'

'Listen, Bass. I broke away from my guards comin' here from Mohave County. I'll do it again if I have the chance.'

'Keno!'

'Give out.'

Eccles squatted beside Boone. 'I'm supposed to leave here in two weeks. I ain't. I'm leaving here day after tomorrow. Oh, it'll be legal enough. They won't come after me.'

'You sound like Pedro Loco.'

Fear welled up in the dark eyes. 'I'm all

right. I kin work it so's you can go with me.'

Boone ground out his smoke. 'You interest me.'

'Then shut up and listen!' Eccles came closer. 'I kin get yuh outa here back into Cell Two with me. Leave it to me. Fact is, I got to leave here without anybody outside knowin' it. The best bet is the river.'

A guard tramped into the entranceway, looked in on them and then walked away again.

Eccles grinned. 'You sit tight. I'll get yuh outa here with me in Cell Two. Until then keep your big mouth shut.'

'I'm dumb, *amigo.*'

Boone studied the outlaw. Dobie had been right when he had said Eccles had connections. Maybe better connections than Jim had realized.

CHAPTER EIGHT

Boone was alone in the Snake Den. Bass Eccles had been returned to Cell Two.

Boone rolled the last smoke from the supply Eccles had left him. He knew the country well from the Salt clear down to the northern reaches of Sonora, but Bass Eccles didn't know that. Some of Eccles' conver-

93

sation had revealed an amazing knowledge of the owlhoot trails of the territory and Sonora. Now and then he had dropped names; names Boone had recognized as men powerful in Arizona politics. The sly-eyed outlaw had a mind honed to a razor-edge, hiding it behind a shield of assumed ignorance, for the man could hardly read or write.

Eccles had been raised in and around Tombstone. His knowledge of Sonora was amazing. He spoke easily of Red Lopez, the *revolutionario* of Fronteras, whose exploits had turned both Sonora and Arizona into a turmoil. He was an *amigo* of bloodthirsty Augustin Chacon, a pure quill *bandido* whose life Eccles had saved by springing him from the Tombstone *calabozo*. The one thing that had impressed Boone was that Eccles was so damned sure of himself.

A guard opened the cell door and looked down at Boone. 'Your time is up in here,' he said.

It was the man named Martin, who seemed to be on friendly terms with Eccles.

'How so?' asked Boone.

Martin grinned. 'You saved a man's life in here. Cap Ingalls is getting worried about the record of this place. Besides, we heard that Yates went after you and you was defending yourself in the craphouse.' Martin unlocked the leg irons.

Boone rubbed his leg and got up. Martin

94

followed him out into the sunny prison yard. 'Eccles and his *amigos* are workin' down in the cemetery. Go down and give him a hand.'

'No guard?' asked Boone in feigned surprise.

Martin glanced up at the tower over the cistern. 'You ever see a man get hit with one of them slugs from that Gatling? Them .45-500 slugs hit like a mule. Ranges up to two miles. I've seen that thing fire up to twelve hundred shots a minute if it's served right.'

'You win.'

'We usually do,' said Martin dryly.

Boone passed through the gate and walked down the slope to the cemetery. Bass Eccles was seated on a rock watching Thalus Hastings, Concho Bates and Benny Hatch working sorking on two graves. He grinned slyly as he saw Boone. 'Told yuh you'd get out, didn't I?'

'Sure did, Bass. What do I do?'

'Set. The boys will be done pretty soon.'

Concho wiped the sweat from his face. 'Grab this Irish banjo, Shattuck.'

Boone looked at Eccles. Eccles grinned. 'Keep goin' Concho,' he said.

Concho thrust out his square jaw. 'You ain't done a tap, Bass. He ain't gettin' outa this, too!'

'By grab, Concho,' Eccles said. 'Yuh talk as though you was the hairy bear in Cell Two. Now that ain't right, is it.'

Concho went back to work, fury in his dark eyes.

Bass spoke in a low voice. 'Everything is set, Boone. Tomorrow night.'

'I'm not too hot about it. The chances are too long.'

'Listen! I told yuh I'd do it.'

'I still don't know why you want me to go along.'

The lean face broke into an infectious, friendly grin. 'How you talk! I like yuh, Boone.'

Boone looked up at the prison, broiling under the hot sun. 'I still can't see how you'll do it.'

Eccles waved a hand. 'Martin is corridor guard tonight and tomorrow night. No moon. Tomorrow night about eleven o'clock you get sick. Leave the rest up to me. Act it up, *amigo*. Mebbe appendicitis. Grip your belly and howl like a coyote.'

Boone nodded.

Thalus Hastings got out of the grave they were working in. 'Pedro Loco will sleep well here,' he said. 'Poor bastard won't be haunted anymore.'

'Yuh talk like a damned sky pilot,' growled Concho.

'How would you know?' asked Eccles. 'Yuh never listened to one in your whole misbegotten life.'

'Go to hell!'

They trudged up the slope to the gate and passed in. Boone looked back just before the guard closed the gate. The Colorado washed the sandy shores below them, yellow and swift, a treacherous flood. Bass had mentioned swimming. Surely he didn't intend to cross that murderous riot.

The cell was pitch dark. Boone lay on his back looking up at the ceiling he could not see. It was close to eleven o'clock. He reached up his hand from the upper bunk he had occupied since Bass Eccles had come back to Cell Two. His fingers traced the deeply cut letters inscribed by Jesus Diaz half a year before. *Libertad!* Jesus had reached liberty all right.

Gentle snoring came from Benny Hatch's bunk. Thalus Hastings groaned in his sleep. A hand gripped Boone's right wrist. It was the signal.

Boone gripped his belly and groaned loudly. He groaned again and then cried in simulated pain. The cry echoed from the arched ceiling.

Thalus Hastings called out. 'What is it, Boone?'

'My guts! That damned prison slop!' He yelled again.

Boots pounded in the corridor. Eccles slid from his bunk and lit a candle. Benny Hatch and Concho Bates looked up at Boone.

97

Boone doubled up and yelled like a Comanche in the full of the moon.

Martin looked in through the double doors. 'What the hell is goin' on in there?'

'Shattuck is sick,' said Eccles.

Thalus Hastings pulled himself up beside Boone. 'Where does it hurt?'

Boone wordlessly pointed to his lower right side.

'Appendicitis, I'll bet,' Hastings said.

Martin unlocked the doors and came in. He looked at Boone. 'Better get you to the infirmary.'

Hastings and Eccles helped Boone down. He doubled over and gripped his gut. Martin stood aside. 'You help him there, Eccles,' he said.

'I hope the bastard dies!' yelled Dixie Yates from the next cell.

'Up your butt!' yelled Concho.

A lantern cast a sickly light. Eccles helped Boone through the ponderous corridor gate. Martin came up behind them. 'The gate guard is in the can,' he said softly. Boone walked beside Eccles toward the gate that overlooked the cemetery. They stopped near the gate. It was pitch black. Eccles gripped Boone by the arm. 'You ready, Martin?' he asked.

'Shoot!'

Eccles smashed a hard blow to Martin's jaw. The guard went down as though poleaxed. Eccles took the keys, opened the gate and shoved Boone through. Eccles closed and locked the barred gate and threw the keys back into the prison yard. 'Come on.' He set off through the darkness like a great lean cat.

The prison was as silent as the grave. Any second Boone expected to hear the chattering roar of the deadly Gatling searching the darkness. Eccles slid down into a gully and started through the scrub trees, then stopped. 'Wait here.' He vanished into the darkness. He was back in a few minutes. 'The boat is there, all right. Come on.'

Boone followed Eccles through the brush. Eccles stepped into a small flat-bottomed skiff. 'Untie it,' he said, 'shove off.'

Eccles took the oars as Boone waded into the water shoving the boat off. He stepped in. 'Take an oar,' said Eccles. They kept in the backwater, rowing steadily against the strong current, heading north.

Boone glanced at his silent companion. 'How the hell did you do it?' he asked wonderingly.

'Shut up and row!'

Twenty minutes drifted past. Behind them lights sprang up on Prison Hill. 'They're wise now,' said Eccles. 'Strip off your pants.'

Boone stripped off his trousers.

'Wedge them under the seat.'

Boone did as he was told. Eccles looked

over his shoulder. 'Row for that sand spit,' he said.

The skiff grounded. They got out. Eccles stripped off his clothing and shoved it under the rear seat. He threw the oars into the dark waters and then waded out with the empty skiff. He turned it over and shoved it out into the strong current. He waded back to shore. 'Get some brush,' he said. 'We'll wipe out our tracks.'

They crossed the spit, wiping out their tracks. On the north side of the spit another skiff was hidden in the brush. Eccles pulled a bundle from under the seat. 'Clothes.' He handed Boone a rough shirt and a pair of trousers, swiftly donning his own. 'Get in.'

Boone clambered into the skiff. Eccles carefully erased their tracks. He got into the skiff and shoved off. 'Row,' he said.

They pulled away from the dim spit, against the current, heading north as before. Boone looked at the silent man beside him. Eccles knew what he was doing.

The dawn was graying the Eastern sky when Eccles turned the skiff in toward a low island that bordered the eastern shore. 'Get rocks,' said Eccles. 'We gotta sink this tub.'

'Why? We can't make it across the desert on foot!'

Eccles' eyes were icy-cold in the graying light. 'I got yuh out, didn't I? Get rocks!'

They loaded the shallow skiff until it was

100

almost awash. Eccles waded out into the stream and sank the boat. He waded back.' 'Get into the brush,' he said. 'We got a long wait. I'll sleep for a spell. You keep watch.' The outlaw curled up on the cold sands and went instantly to sleep.

Late in the afternoon, Boone saw dust on the east bank below them. Eccles was on his second shift of sleep. Boone gripped the outlaw's shoulder. Eccles opened his eyes. Boone pointed at the dust. Three horsemen appeared. 'Yumas,' said Bass.

The trackers rode slowly north, studying the ground. They passed the island. Boone glanced at Eccles. The man's face was white and set, almost as it had been the night Pedro Loco had almost killed him. The trackers disappeared to the north. Eccles yawned. 'We're all right now,' he said.

Boone was in a fitful sleep when Eccles shook him awake. 'Listen,' he said.

Deep shadows bordered the river. The sun was gone, dying behind the Picachos on the California shore. Down the river there came a thudding noise and the faint splash of water. 'Steamer,' said Bass. 'Take off your shoes.'

Boone wordlessly pulled off his prison shoes.

'Throw them far out,' said Eccles as he

heaved his footgear out into the shadowy waters. Boone followed suit. Lights showed down the river and they saw the dim white bulk of a stern-wheeler, forging against the yellow current with a steady *frash, frash, frash* of paddles. Eccles grinned at Boone. 'I hope to God you wasn't lyin' about bein' able to swim. Help me shove this log into the rio.'

They manhandled the thick timber into the water and began to swim, hooking an arm over the log. The steamer was forging slowly upstream. The rio was dark now, shadowed by the western bluffs. Eccles looked at Boone. 'We let go of the log when she's a hundred yards away. By grab, we gotta keep away from them paddles!'

The thudding of the engine and the thrash of the big paddles echoed from the dark bluffs. The packet forced itself upstream, curling the foam-flecked yellow water back from the low prow.

'Now!' said Eccles. He shoved away from the log. Eccles struggled desperately in the swift current, looked despairingly at Boone. Boone struck out, gripped the tall man across the chest and spoke swiftly, 'Take it easy. Kick with your feet. Don't struggle!'

The steamer was fifty yards away, almost in line with them. Eccles gasped and began to struggle. The overhang of the steamer's deck began to loom over them. Then it was on them. The hull banged against Boone's

102

shoulder. He let go of Eccles. The outlaw went down and came up gasping and spluttering. Boone gripped him by the collar. The hull surged past, washing them up and down. Boone gripped a trailing line and hung on like grim death. The paddles thrashed steadily twenty feet from them. If Boone let go they would be swept under forever.

A head appeared over the low rail. A pair of arms reached past Boone and gripped the gasping Eccles by the shirt. Then Eccles was over the rail, kicking hard. One of his feet struck Boone on the head and pushed hard. Boone went under, clinging to the rope. He came up, spitting out silty water.

Eccles was on the deck. The man with him gripped Boone and pulled him up. Boone sprawled on the wet deck, gasping for air. The man jerked his head. 'Come on.' They followed him into a small cabin. He locked the door and turned up the light. 'Right on time, Bass,' he said with a grin.

Bass began to strip off his wet clothing. 'Take a look around the deck, Frank.'

Bass locked the door behind him. 'Strip,' he said. He took clothes from a pile on the bunk and threw them onto a chair near Boone.

Boone jerked his head toward the door. 'Who's he?'

'Cousin. Frank Moran.'

Boone eyed the shivering man with admiration. 'How do you do it, Bass?'

'Easy. I'll tell yuh once we get off the steamer. She'll tie up for the night a couple miles north of here. We'll stay on all day tomorrow. By that time we'll be a helluva a ways upriver. We'll leave the steamer when she reaches Ehrenberg.'

In dry clothing, Bass dropped on the bunk. 'Frank got the job as cook on here a month ago. Sure handy, wasn't it?'

'Bass, you're a genius.'

Bass waved a hand. 'Connections.'

Frank called through the door. 'All clear, Bass!'

Boone let the man in. Frank took a bottle from a drawer and handed it to Bass. Bass drank deeply and handed it to Boone. 'By grab, I needed that. What's the news from Yuma, Frankie?'

'They found Phil Martin with a busted jaw lyin' near the gate. Trackers started up and down the river. Some of them found an overturned skiff with prison clothes in it. They figgered yuh drownded.'

'Damn near did.' Bass laughed. 'Busted Martin's jaw! Hawww! Some joke on him.'

'Sure is,' said Boone. He took a stiff hooker.

Frank took a drink. 'I'll get you some chuck. We ain't carryin' no passengers this trip. Just army stores for Fort Mohave. No one will bother yuh in here so long as yuh keep quiet.'

104

'Keno,' said Bass.

Frank left the cabin. Eccles lay back luxuriously. 'Travelin' in style,' he said. 'This is my speed. While them dumb bastards back there think we drownded. Hawww!'

Boone rolled a smoke from a sack of makings on a small table and eyed Eccles. He was damned sure Eccles had tried to push him under after Eccles was safe on deck. The cold-gutted shark was as treacherous as an Apache.

Eccles fell asleep. He slept as peacefully as though he had done an honest day's work.

Ehrenberg was a cluster of yellow lights on the west bank. The river was dark as the *Yavapai* neared the little river port. 'Half a mile, Bass,' Boone said.

'Keno.' Bass shoved a bottle into his coat pocket and slid a Colt six-shooter under his belt. He placed his hat on his bald head. 'Dark enough to get off without bein' seen?'

'Yes.'

'Bueno!'

Frank stuck his head into the cabin. 'Get aft,' he said. 'Jump off as soon as we dock.'

'You comin' along?' asked Bass.

'Hell no!' said Frank. 'I'll quit when we get to Fort Mohave.'

'O.K. I'll send the money to you at Prescott like we agreed.'

Frank nodded. 'Don't you cross me, Bass,'

he warned.

Bass looked surprised. 'Who? Me? Why, Frank!'

'Just you have the money there.'

'It'll be there. Ain't we cousins?'

'You'd double-cross your grandmother for a plug of spit-or-drown, you baldheaded bastard.' Frank vanished.

Bass grinned. 'Ain't he the one though?'

The steamer slowed down as it edged in. She bumped gently against the rough pilings. Bass darted from the cabin, leaped ashore and jumped behind a pile of freight. Boone crouched beside him. Bass peered over the boxes. 'All clear. Leg it.'

They ran into a dark alleyway and headed west through the little adobe town. At the outskirts Bass snatched a canteen hanging from a *jacal* wall and filled it at a well. They faded into the dimness of the desert night, slogging through the sand away from the Wickenburg road.

At the end of an hour Bass stopped and dropped to the ground. He took a hard biscuit from his pocket and handed it to Boone.

Boone gnawed at the biscuit. 'If it ain't askin' too much,' he said, 'what the hell are we doin' out here?'

Bass finished his biscuit and rolled a smoke. 'We've done all right so far, haven't we?'

'You sure as hell don't let a body into your plans.'

The dark eyes were half-veiled. 'I been gettin' by forty years thataway. You just keep your mouth shut and string along with old Bass Eccles, sonny. I ain't forgot you saved my life twice. Old Bass don't forget them things!'

They kept on, trending to the south-east. It was well after midnight when Bass stopped and took a stiff slug from his bottle. He passed it to Boone. 'We'd best get some sleep,' he said. The lean outlaw seemed to be composed of whang leather and forged metal.

Several hours before dawn Eccles got up and shook Boone awake. They started off again, through low hills, hardly visible in the darkness. Suddenly Boone raised his head. 'Smoke,' he said.

Boone scanned the darkness with his eyes. There was nothing to see except the low humped hills. Eccles gripped Boone's arm. 'Stay here,' he said. He vanished. Boone squatted wearily. His feet were molded into one mass with his shoes and socks. Blisters had burst and pasted his socks to his raw flesh.

Eccles materialized in the night. 'Come on,' he said. 'It's all right.' He led the way between high walls of rock. Then they were in a wide cup of rock. A man was squatting by a fire, feeding mesquite branches into it. His high Mex sombrero cast a grotesque shadow on the rock wall behind him. A bedding roll lay to one side. A horse nickered as Boone and Bass approached the fire. There were three of them picketed beyond the fire.

The man at the fire turned. 'Hola, Bass,' he said.

'*Companero,*' said Bass. '*Como esta?*'

'Good, my cousin,' the man said in fluid Spanish. 'I am here as you asked.'

Boone looked into a broad, flat face, the Indian strong in it. The eyes were flat and expressionless like those of a snake. A cartridge belt crossed the broad chest. The butt of a nickel-plated pistol showed from a carved leather holster.

Bass turned. 'This my friend Boone,' he said in Spanish to the Mexican. 'Boone Shattuck. Boone, this is my cousin, Bartolome Huerta. One of the true girt.'

Boone felt his skin crawl. This was the man Eccles was supposed to have double-crossed along with Sim Bellam and Dance Younger. Bartolome Huerta, the *ladrone* from Nacozari. 'How is it with you, Bartolome?' he said in cowpen Spanish.

'Very well, friend. There is food. There are horses and guns as you asked, Bass.'

'Good!'

Huerta's face was pocked with smallpox pits. A thick scar showed on the upper lip, leaving a bare patch in his heavy mustache. He removed a pot from the embers.

'Mex strawberries and tortillas,' said Bass.

'Tequila also,' said Huerta over his shoulder.

Boone sat down on a rock. 'How long has he been here?'

'Three days,' said Huerta.

Boone looked at Bass. 'Three horses. He expected someone to come with you.'

'All he knew was that I wouldn't be alone.'

'Who was coming with you if I hadn't come?'

'Concho Bates. Hawww!'

'Why didn't you take him instead of me?'

Bass sipped the tequila. 'Yuh saved my life. Besides, I never trusted Concho like I do you, *amigo.*'

I'll bet you do, thought Boone. He helped himself to tequila. 'I'd still like to know how you did it.'

Bass watched Bartolome ladle beans into tin plates. 'Yeh. Yuh see, Boone, I got connections. *High* connections. They *had* to let me get outa Yuma before my time was up.'

'How so?'

'I could have talked plenty about things that happened some years ago. The Tucson Ring. You've heard of it?'

'Some,' admitted Boone.

'Well, I did some work for the boys years ago. I was on the inside in a lot of deals.

109

Then when some of the boys got into big jobs they wanted to forget how they got started, and forget old Bass also. But old Bass didn't forget. He had a report writ out and sent copies to some of the boys. The other copy was kept hid. I told the boys that report would be turned over to the authorities unless I got help.'

'I'm beginning to get it.'

They began to eat, scooping the hot beans up with folds of tortilla. Bass talked steadily. 'I had enemies waitin' for me to be released. Why, hellsfire, they woulda been breathin' down my neck all the way to Willcox. Now, old Bass wants to live a good life from now on.'

'On the *hacienda?*'

Huerta glanced quickly at Boone.

Bass nodded. 'So I worked out this deal. I figgered I'd better make things look like I escaped. That was why I needed you, Boone. Now, with them findin' that overturned skiff and them prison clothes, they'll think we drownded. Frank got in touch with me a couple days afore we escaped. Frank placed the skiffs for us.'

'You've got some handy cousins.'

'Yeh. Yeh. Hawww!'

Boone placed his plate on the ground. Huerta threw him a blanket. Boone rolled up in the blanket, and lay there listening to the low voices of Eccles and Huerta.

110

The flat crack of a gun awoke Boone. He threw aside his blanket and instinctively rolled behind a rock. Bass Eccles laughed. 'You're as touchy as a virgin,' he said. The outlaw stood beyond the smoking fire holding a six-gun in his hand. 'I was just tryin' my hand again on my six-guns. Bartolome brought them for me.'

Bass wore a buscadero belt, heavy with the weight of holsters and guns. 'I'm tryin' out my old *dinero* winning stunt. Watch.'

The empty tequila bottle hung from a string tied to a projecting rock, thirty feet away from Bass. He settled his gunbelt about his lean hips and then snapped his hands down for a double draw. The right hand Colt came up, steadied and then flamed. Nothing happened. Bass slid the Colts back into their holsters. Again he went into a crouch and double draw. The righthand Colt roared. The string snapped. Before the bottle hit the ground the lefthand Colt splattered it through the morning air.

'Bueno!' said Bartolome. He suspended another bottle. Bass eyed Boone. 'You want to try it?'

Boone shook his head. 'I'm just average with a six-gun.'

'Bass is the best,' Bartolome said. 'With six-gun or rifle. With the knife he is almost as good as Bartolome Huerta.'

Boone washed in a shallow *tinaja*. Letters

111

were cut into the rock wall behind the water pan. 'L. Biggins,' he read, 'passed here in '67. Mohaves on trail. May God help me.' Higher up were the initials R.O. and the date of 1858. To one side was a line of sharply incised letters in wavering Spanish. 'There is nothing but death here in this accursed land. 1705.'

'The ancient ones,' said Bartolome quietly. 'Several times I have seen such inscriptions. At Tinajas Atlas, the High Tanks, near the fearful Camino del Diablo. The Devil's Road, far to the south in Sonora.'

Bass was saddling a gray. 'Take the buckskin,' he said to Boone.

'I'll need a gun,' Boone said.

'I always carry two six-guns and a Winchester. You'll get a gun if you need it.'

'You've got the Colt Frank gave you.'

'So I have.'

'I'll take it.'

'It's got a rocking cylinder.'

'I'll take it anyway.'

Bass glanced at Bartolome. 'All right.' He took the old Colt from a saddlebag and handed it to Boone. Boone checked it. The cylinder was a little loose. It had five rounds in it.

He thrust it under his belt.

CHAPTER NINE

They had passed through the Kofas, skirted the Mineral Springs, crossed the Southern Pacific tracks and the Gila, and had gone into camp five miles from Gila Bend. Bass lay on his blanket, looking up at the ice-chip stars. 'One of us oughta go into Gila Bend and nose around,' he said.

'Not me,' said Bartolome. 'I am known too well there.'

'I ain't about to go,' said Bass. 'I'm goin' all the way to the San Pedro and beyond by the back trails. How about you goin' in, Boone?'

An idea struck him. 'I might be spotted,' he said.

'Sho! Sneak in, get some grub, and sneak out again.'

'I don't like it, Bass.'

'Saddle up,' he said. 'We'll wait here.'

'To hell with it!'

Eccles sat up, cold fury on his face. 'Git! You ride with me, you learn to take orders!'

'Si!' said Bartolome.

'All right,' he said, 'don't get on the prod.'

'You'll learn,' said Bass.

Boone saddled his horse. Bass threw him a

113

money pouch. 'Bring a couple bottles,' he said. 'Cartridges. Coffee. Flour. Tobacco.'

He rode slowly into town. The town was busy, and Boone suddenly realized it was Saturday night. Wagons and buckboards lined the main street. Boone tethered the buckskin to a rack at the edge of town and walked east along the main street. Boone wouldn't put it past Bass to trail him or send Bartolome along after him.

Boone made his purchases in a small general store and took them back to the horse. He tied the sack to the saddle and then remembered that Bass had asked for liquor. He walked to the nearest saloon. Boone stepped up on the porch and looked into the saloon. It was busy. He walked in, passed behind the men at the bar and stopped at the counter near the rear. 'Two bottles of rye,' he said to the barkeep.

'I see you've turned to heavy drinking,' a familiar voice said.

Boone turned to look into the humorous eyes of Jim Dobie. 'You do move around,' he said.

'No more than you. I didn't know you had gotten this far.'

'You knew we made the break?'

'Yes. One of our men wired at once. You're supposed to be drowned.'

'Where can I talk to you?'

'I've got a room at the hotel. First on the

114

right, top of the stairs.'

'Keno. Go there.'

Dobie left and Boone followed him. He stood for a time in the alleyway watching the street crowd and then he went up the stairs and rapped on the door. Dobie opened it and locked it behind Boone. 'Well?'

Boone swiftly told him of what had happened.

'It seems as though we underestimated Brother Eccles. I quit my job in Willcox and came here, poking about for news. We didn't know Huerta was in the Territory.'

'Don't make any moves until I find that damned gold.'

'I won't.'

'What's new in Willcox?'

'Dowling was ousted. He spends his time in the cribs, getting a big rake-off. Eli Bell was appointed marshal.'

'A good man.'

'Maybe. Eli looks out for himself.'

'Where are Bellam and Younger?'

'Younger was at his ranch the last I knew. Bellam has vanished.'

'I thought, from what you told me that Huerta was down on Eccles, but they seem to be real *amigos*. They're cousins.'

Dobie nodded. 'Huerta's mother and Eccles' mother are sisters. I found that out after you left. From Jonce Maxon.'

Boone raised his head. 'How is Jonce?'

Dobie grinned. 'You mean Marion, don't you?'

'Well?'

'Jonce has been damned sick. Marion has been in town several times for medicine. She asked Eli Bell how you were.'

Boone rubbed his jaw. 'I know little more about the gold than I did when I went into Yuma.'

'At least you're companeros with Eccles and Huerta.'

'Yeh,' said Boone dryly. 'I sure am.'

Dobie said, 'I have something of yours here.' He thrust his hand into a saddlebag and brought out Boone's Sheriff's Model Colt and the bellygun.

Boone handed the single-action back to Dobie. 'Keep this.' He slid the bellygun into his coat pocket. 'Eccles wants to keep me at a disadvantage.'

'You can pull out, Boone.'

Boone shook his head.

Dobie handed him his Wells-Fargo badge and papers. Boone stood up. 'I'd better get back,' he said.

'What do you want me to do?'

Boone shrugged. 'I think we're heading for the Willcox area. Beyond that I know nothing.'

'I'll go back there.'

'It's about all you can do.'

Boone left the hotel by a back door and

went to the buckskin. Bass was asleep when Boone returned. Huerta took one of the bottles and drank deeply. Boone unsaddled the buckskin and picketed him. He was about to go back to the fire when he noticed Huerta's claybank. The horse had been picketed at the edge of the hollow when Boone had left. Now he was on the far side of the depression. His saddle had been near the fire. Now it was lying beneath a mesquite bush. Boone went back to the fire and rolled a smoke. Eccles snored steadily.

Huerta lay back against his bedroll, drinking steadily, watching Boone whenever Boone looked away.

The lights of a ranch showed through the moonlight a mile away. Somewhere behind Boone a coyote raised his melancholy voice. A cold wind searched through the draws, rustling the brush. Bartolome leaned on his rifle twenty feet away looking toward the ranch. He held the reins of his horse and that of Bass Eccles. The tall outlaw had vanished into the moonlit brush.

Behind them lay the long trail from Gila Bend. They had traveled at night through the Maricopas to Johnson's Well, from there across Santa Rosa Wash, to the Santa Cruz. There Bass had left them to return a day later. From there they had crossed the Tucson-Nogales Road, angling south-east to the San Pedro, and then through the brooding Dragoons to where they were now.

'Where has he gone?' asked Boone of the silent breed.

Huerta shrugged. *'Quien sabe?'*

'You know!'

'Perhaps. What difference does it make, *amigo?* An escaped prisoner need not know anything except that he is safe for the time being,' Huerta said in Spanish.

The long night rides and the hidden camps had worked on Boone's nerves, honing them thin.

Eccles padded back through the silvery moonlight. 'O.K.,' he said, 'let's go. We kin sleep in a bed tonight at least.'

They rode down toward the ranch. As they drew near Boone could see the loop-holed adobe and stone buildings on a slight rise. Eccles dismounted behind the house. A tall, gangling man shambled out of the shadows. 'Yuh kin put the horses in the barn,' he said. 'Best to leave them saddled. Yuh kin sleep in the 'dobe down in the hollow. We got vittles areadyin'.'

Boone stared. It was Jonce Maxon.

They led the horses into the barn. Eccles slapped the dust from his rough clothing. 'Lady in there,' he said with a smirk.

Maxon looked at Boone. 'Shattuck,' he said nervously. 'I didn't know you knew Eccles!' Maxon turned. 'This man is wanted for robbery,' he said. 'You didn't tell me he escaped from Yuma with you!'

'What's the difference, Maxon?'

'He's wanted, I tell yuh!'

Eccles grinned. 'So is Bartolome. So am I.'

Maxon wiped his ravaged face. 'How long will yuh stay here?'

'Until my business is done.'

Maxon lowered his voice. 'I got a rumor that there have been some Wells-Fargo men pokin' about.'

Eccles' lopsided grin vanished and a cold look came into his eyes. 'Who are they?'

Maxon shrugged. 'I don't know.'

Eccles gripped the tall man by his corded throat and slammed him back against the wall. 'You sure?'

'I swear to God, I don't know?'

'How'd yuh find out?'

'Eli Bell.'

'How'd he find out?'

'When he took over as marshal in Willcox he found a badge in the desk. Locked in, it was. A Wells-Fargo badge. Bell left it there. Coupla nights later it was gone.'

'Who took it?'

'He don't know for sure. But Jim Dobie quit as jailor. He took his stuff from the cala-bozo. The badge was missing after that.'

'Who's Dobie?'

'Who knows? Came in Willcox a couple months ago from New Mexico. Got the

119

jailor's job. He was the man swore that Shattuck there didn't kill Cass Caston, only Billy Steen. It saved Shattuck from a rope, I tell yuh.'

Eccles released the shaking rancher and turned slowly to look at Boone. Huerta slid around behind Boone.

'Dobie saw the whole hassle,' Boone said easily. 'He testified at the inquest. What's wrong with that?'

'Nothin',' said Eccles softly. '*Amigo* of yours?'

'No. Never saw him until I came to Willcox.'

'That so? Yuh think he's Wells-Fargo?'

'How the hell should I know?'

Eccles slid a hand down to his hand Colt. Boone turned so that he could see both Huerta and Eccles. He slowly opened his coat, revealing the old Colt in his belt.

Eccles eyed the Colt. 'Where is this hombre Dobie now, Jonce?'

'He left Willcox three-four days ago. On the S.P. travelin' west.'

'Where was he headin'?'

'I don't know.'

Eccles rubbed his lean jaw. 'Well, we better get some chuck. How's Marion, Jonce?'

Jonce flushed. 'All right. It was on account of her Shattuck got into trouble with Steen and Caston.'

Eccles cold eyes studied Boone. 'So?'

120

Boone shrugged. 'They were chousin' her. I stepped in.'

'God,' said Eccles shaking his head.

Boone slipped his hand into his left-hand pocket and felt the smooth butt of his hide-out gun. 'Just like I stepped in when Pedro Loco was whipping you all to hell, Eccles. Maybe I should've kept out of that too.'

'Damn you. You watch that lip, Shattuck.'

'You watch yours, Eccles. I'm not hankerin' to ride the rio with you and listen to your yappin'. You get to hell outa my way, I'll leave.'

Eccles paled. 'Where do you think you're goin'?'

'Sonora maybe.'

'No you ain't. You know too damned much.'

Boone's voice was low and steady. 'Listen, Eccles, I appreciate what you did for me. I played my part helping you in the rid. Call it quits.'

'Yuh seen what I did to that bottle in the Kofas.'

Boone grinned.

Maxon wet his lips. 'I don't want no trouble, Bass.'

The outlaw suddenly grinned. 'Hellsfire, guess we're all tired out, Boone. Fergit it, will yuh?'

Maxon smiled uneasily. 'Yeh. We got a bait of meat cookin' for you boys. Let's get into the house and take care of it.'

'Sure,' said Bass. 'That's the way. Go ahead, Boone!'

'Why, after *you*, Bass, you're the boss!'

'All right, Boone.' Eccles left the barn.

Huerta stopped beside Boone. 'I did not like the way you spoke to Bass,' he said thinly.

Boone eyed the Mexican. 'So?'

Huerta tapped Boone on the chest with a thick hand. 'Do not do it again, hombre.'

Boone slapped down the hand and stepped in close. 'Get into the house, you bastard. I've taken enough lip from Bass without having to take it from you.'

Huerta jumped aside. His right hand slid beneath his coat and swept out with a thin-bladed *cuchillo*. Boone snatched a bucket from a hook and threw it at the Mexican. The bottom rim caught Huerta on the chin. He went down hard, blood splattering from his smashed chin. Boone picked up the *cuchillo* and thrust it in between two boards, snapped the blade and threw the pieces on top of the Mexican.

The big kitchen was redolent with the odors of hot food. Eccles sat at the table. 'Where's Bartolome?' he asked Boone.

'He'll be along.'

Eccles studied Boone. 'You feelin' all right?'

Boone grinned. 'Sure. Why not?'

'You look like you swallowed the canary.'

A woman entered the kitchen. Boone looked up into the eyes of Marion Maxon. She stepped back and glanced from Boone to Eccles. 'Hello, Marion,' said Boone.

'I thought you were in Yuma,' she said quietly.

'I was.'

Eccles laughed. 'Boone and me left Yuma. We got tired of it.'

Jonce Maxon loosened his collar. 'I'll stay outside, Bass.'

'Why?'

'Somebody's got to keep an eye open.'

Eccles leaned back in his chair. 'What's wrong with you, Jonce?'

Jonce did not answer. Marion spoke. 'I'll tell you what's wrong! Three outlaws coming here. Supposing the sheriff finds out?'

Eccles' eyes went cold. 'I've done Jonce many a favor. The least he can do is put us up for a time.'

'We'll feed you and then you can leave.'

'We'll leave when we're damned good and ready! You open your mouth about us bein' here and your father will suffer. You can bet on that, sister.'

The door opened and Bartolome Huerta staggered in, holding his bloody chin. 'What the hell happened to you?' asked Bass.

Huerta looked at Boone. Bass whirled. 'You!'

Boone nodded. 'You tell that cousin of

123

yours that I don't take any lip from him. He pulled a knife on me.'

Eccles stood up. 'Lord! What have I got myself into?'

'Nothing,' said Boone. 'That Mex goes for me again and I'll kill him.'

Jonce Maxon put on his hat and left the kitchen. Marion turned away as the Mexican dabbled at the blood on his chin. There was naked hate in Huerta's eyes. Now he would have to be constantly on guard against the Mexican.

Eccles leaned across the table. 'Mebbe I oughta get rid of yuh!'

Boone shrugged.

'You'd like that, wouldn't yuh?'

'I'll stick,' Boone said.

'Mebbe I shoulda taken Concho Bates along after all.'

'It's a little late now, isn't it?'

Their eyes clashed and Eccles looked away. 'Wash off that chin, Bartolome,' he said. 'You two *hombres* forget what happened. One more thing like this and I'll take a hand in it.'

Huerta left the room and they could hear him splashing water in the bucket outside the door. Eccles grinned. 'You're a fighter from who laid the chunk, Boone,' he said easily. 'Too bad you ain't got the brains to go with it.'

'Like you.'

'Yeh. *Like me.*'

They ate silently. The Mexican shoved back his plate and left the kitchen. Eccles said, 'I'll get some sleep. You take the first watch, Boone.' He left.

Marion began to clear the table. 'They're no good,' she said. 'Leave at once. It's dangerous here.'

'What do you mean?'

She glanced at the rear door. 'Sheriff Kelly was here a few days ago. He'll be back. Get out of here while you have the chance.'

'Why are you telling me this?'

She turned. 'You can get into Mexico easily from here. It's less than forty miles. Please go.'

'I won't as long as Eccles is here.'

The hazel eyes held his. 'There will be bloodshed here if you don't.'

Boone stood up. 'I'm staying.'

'I warned you.'

Boone opened the door. 'You and your father can leave. Go to Willcox or Benson.'

She shook her head. 'He's ill. This is his home. No one will drive us from it.'

Boone heard her sob as he closed the door.

CHAPTER TEN

A faint moon silvered the desert and streamed in through the narrow windows of the old adobe. Boone lay with his eyes open. He could hear the steady breathing of Bass Eccles across the room. There was no sound in Huerta's room, just beyond theirs.

Boone swung his legs and placed his feet on the cold floor. He took his old Colt and walked to the door of Huerta's room. The sagging cot was empty, the blanket lying on the littered floor. Boone padded back across his room. Something scraped the wall near the window. Boone stepped into the shadows, waiting.

An arm came through the narrow window. A head appeared. It was Huerta. The Mexican stared at Boone's empty cot. Then he looked quickly about the little room and withdrew his head. His feet pattered on the hard earth.

Bass Eccles moved. Boone whirled. 'What did you expect?' Eccles asked in a low voice.

Boone sat down, away from the window. 'I guess I was wrong in flattening him,' he said.

'Damned fool Texan! Along the border here we don't boot them around like they

126

do along the Rio Grande.'

'They do a little booting themselves where I come from.'

Bass stood up and walked into Huerta's room. He shut the door behind him. There was the sound of angry voices and then low talking. Feet scraped on the floor. Then the outer door banged shut. Bass came back into the room and dropped on his bunk.

'Well?' asked Boone.

'I've sent him south.'

'Why?'

'I need both of you proddy *hombres*. Right now we can't afford to have trouble.'

Hoofs thudded. Boone stood up and looked through the window. Huerta was riding south.

Bass lay back on his bunk. 'We'll be headin' across the border before long.'

Boone eased his hand down to his Colt. 'Why Mexico? The Ruales ain't exactly happy to have *ladinos* like us under foot.'

'I got friends down in Sonora. In Durango, too. We'll be all right.'

'Yeh. Without *dinero*. I don't like it here, Bass. Why are we hanging around?'

Bass spoke slowly. 'We don't have to worry about *dinero*. I can get all we'll need. Trouble is, I can't get it alone. I need help. You're elected.'

Boone eyed the shadowy figure. 'Where is it?'

127

'One thing you got to get through that thick head of yours. You're too proddy. You act like you got a bug up your butt. Now you either take orders, or you can fork your hoss and dust up the road. But you won't get far. Every county law officer is on the lookout for yuh.'

'We drowned. Remember?'

'Yeh. But I'm not sure they swallowed that. Mebbe somebody will talk. You either stick with old Bass or you'll be back in Yuma and this time they'll make damned sure you don't break out. You'll spend your time in the Snake Den and end up like Pedro Loco. Now get some sleep. Tomorrow we got work to do.'

Boone lay down, but he kept his hand on his six gun until he was sure Eccles was a asleep again.

Bass Eccles shook Boone awake. 'Get up,' he said, 'Jonce is gone.' The gray light of the false dawn showed in the sky. Eccles' face was dark with fury. 'Mebbe he went into Willcox. I ain't takin' no chances.'

'He hasn't got the guts.'

Eccles shrugged. 'Mebbe. Fact is, Jonce useta be quite a man. *Muy hombre.* Afore he got to gettin' his courage from a whiskey bottle.'

Boone pulled on his boots. 'So what do we do?'

'Get some jamoke. You tail him towards Willcox. One of the vaqueros saw him headin' that way.'

Boone slid his Colt beneath his belt. 'What about you?'

'I'll stay here. You keep an eye on him if you find him.'

'I'm not about to go into Willcox.'

'Yuh don't have to!'

Boone went into the barn and saddled his horse. He went to the house. Marion was in the kitchen serving two vaqueros. They eyed Boone and then left after they finished eating. Boone filled a cup with coffee. 'Where's your father?'

'Gone.'

'Where?'

She eyed him coldly. 'Does he have to leave an account of his whereabouts with you?'

'No! But Bass doesn't like it.'

Her face was flushed. 'Why don't you leave? There will be nothing but trouble with Bass around here. Why don't you leave?'

Boone sipped his coffee. 'We've got business.'

'What kind of business? My father is worried sick. Years ago he would have run Bass into the desert. He was more of a man than you and Bass put together. It's a terrible thing to see the fear in him.'

'He'll be all right.' Boone spoke in a low

voice. 'Please tell me where he has gone. Believe me, nothing will happen to him.'

'I can't understand you.'

He gripped her arm. 'Look. I butted into trouble in Willcox helping you. I want no thanks. But you must trust me a little.'

The hazel eyes held Boone's. 'All right. He's gone to Willcox. He left forty-five minutes ago.'

The door banged open and Eccles came in. 'Get movin', Boone,' he said. He sat down at the table. 'Get me some chuck, Marion.'

Boone saddled his horse and rode out. A mile from the ranch he cut east and followed the base of a ridge where he could see the road. There was no dust on the winding road.

The sun came up. The buckskin plodded steadily along. Then Boone saw the buckboard standing near a wash. There was no one near it. He swung down and ground-reined two hundred yards from the buckboard. Then Boone heard the sound of digging. He walked softly to the edge of the wash. Jonce Maxon was digging steadily below. As Boone watched he saw Jonce reach into the hole and drag out a sack. With shaking hands he pulled out a bottle and uncorked it. The rancher drank deeply and then sat down on the bank of the wash.

'Jonce!'

The rancher whirled and dropped the

bottle as he saw Boone. 'What the hell are you doin' out here?'

'Taking a ride.'

'You're a damned liar!'

Boone walked to the rancher and sat down beside him. Maxon picked up the bottle and took a deep slug. 'Marion don't let me keep the stuff in the house no more,' he said.

'You take any more of that stuff and you'll have a one-way ride to Boot Hill.'

Maxon wiped his shaking hands on his pants. 'I need it.'

'Why? Your ranch is going to pot. Marion is disgusted with you. Bass Eccles has you scared to death. Why?'

'I ain't afraid of him.' Maxon could feel the liquor working in him. 'I'll run him off when I get back.'

'You'll get a slug in your back.'

'Seems as though you know that bastard pretty well. That's *his* way all right. A slug in the back.'

Boone rolled a smoke.

'Give me a quirly,' said Jonce.

Boone handed him the cigarette and lit it for him. 'What's he got on you, Maxon?'

'What's it to you?' Jonce eyed Boone. 'I don't figger you, Shattuck. You seemed like a right nice fella when you helped Marion. By God, I never seen such shootin' when you downed Steen.'

'Yeh, you saw the shooting all right. You

131

sure as hell didn't testify that way at the trial.'

Maxon flushed. 'Yuh got away with it, didn't yuh?'

Boone nodded. 'No thanks to you, Maxon.'

'I don't want trouble. God knows I've had enough of it. Dowling ain't one to fool with. He was out after yuh. He's sore enough at Marion for what she said. He finds out that Bass Eccles and you are at my place, there'll be hell to pay. Dowling ain't yella like Eccles.'

Boone rolled a smoke. 'I didn't know Eccles was yellow.'

'He's as treacherous as an Apache! Him and that Huerta are a pair. Appears to me yuh don't want to live long, Shattuck.'

'He got me out of Yuma.'

'Yeah. For his own ends, he did. Shattuck, if yuh had any sense, you'd pull leather right now and never stop until yuh was out of Arizona!'

Boone grinned. 'Not while Eccles has *dinero* coming.'

The bloodshot eyes studied Boone. 'Yuh know about that?'

'Sure.'

'Blood money.'

'Forty thousand is a lot of blood money.'

'I want no part of it. Not that Eccles would part with any of it.'

'Then why are you helping him?' Boone gripped the man's thin wrist. 'Why?'

132

Maxon looked up. 'Some years ago me and Bass was deputies here in Cochise County. We got full of red-eye. Leastways *I* did. We were assigned as guards on a bullion shipment from Tombstone to Benson. Some miles outa Tombstone the wagon was held up. I was too damned drunk to know what was goin' on. When I comes to I see the wagon standin' in the road. The driver was dead. The bullion was gone, six thousand dollars' worth. Bass was gone too. Out in the brush was a Mex, dead with a hole in the back of his head. I go back to Tombstone. Eccles shows up, claimin' he was disarmed. He claimed three men held up the waggin and he followed them clear down to the border and then lost them. I lost my job. So did Eccles. I tried to clear myself but it was no use.'

Maxon drank deeply. 'The dead Mex was Jorge Huerta. Brother to Bartolome Huerta. Eccles told me I shot him. I was scared to death of Huerta. He's mean as hell. Eccles said he wouldn't say anything to Bartolome. He's held it over my head ever since.'

'You mean that you don't know whether or not you killed Jorge?'

Maxon held up the bottle. 'John Barleycorn entered my mouth as the preachers say, and stole my senses. You know, Shattuck, *I don't know whether I killed Jorge or not!*'

'What do you think?'

133

'I was drunker'n a hoot owl. There was some shooting and then I passed out. Lost a good job. Lost all my friends. My wife never was the same until she died. Marlon never forgave me, but she did stick with me. She's a good girl, Boone.'

'Too damned good for you.'

Maxon drank again. 'I wasn't headin' for Willcox. I don't want Eccles to be on my back.'

Boone shoved back his hat. 'What about the express robbery?'

Maxon shrugged. 'Bellam, Younger and Huerta don't have the brains to pull a job like that. Eccles and Dowling planned it. Eccles alibied for them. Dowling swore they was at Eccles' 'dobe all day. Trouble is, Eccles crossed Dowling. That I know. Mor'n once Dowling has worked me over tryin' to find where the loot was hidden.'

'You know?'

The red eyes steadied on Boone. 'I think so.'

'Where?'

Maxon stood up. 'I'd better get back to the ranch.'

Boone shook his head. 'Take a ride. Go to Dos Cabezas.'

'Why?'

'Do as I say, Maxon, or by God, I'll work you over!'

'All right. All right. I've had enough

trouble. Maybe he'll be gone when I get back.' The rancher filled the earth in on his liquor cache and took his bottle to the buckboard. He got in, slapped the reins on the rumps of his mules and drove slowly north on the dusty road.

Boone walked back to the buckskin and followed the foot of the ridge. He was almost to Dos Cabezas before he turned off. Maxon had done as he had been told.

Boone picketed the buckskin in a small canyon and slept. Then he rode close toward Willcox until he reached Eccles' old adobe. The place was just as it had been when he had first seen it. He found a brushy spot two hundred yards from the adobe and dropped to the warm earth watching it. Hours drifted by.

Boone was dozing when he heard the beat of hoofs to the east. A big man rode a gray horse up, took a spade from the saddle and led the gray to the adobe. It was big Eli Bell. The marshal went into the adobe.

The sun was far down when Bell came out wiping his face and returned to the gray. Then he was gone.

Boone waited twenty minutes and then padded toward the adobe. There was a deep hole just behind the battered stove. Boone rolled a quirly and sat down in a rickety chair. Bell was like everyone else in the Willcox area, determined that the loot was hidden in the adobe.

It was dark when Boone left the adobe and walked toward Willcox.

CHAPTER ELEVEN

The ragged tinkling of a piano came to Boone on the night breeze. He walked down a dark alleyway, past the hurdy-gurdy houses. They were brightly lit and he could hear women's voices mingling with the hoarse voices of drunken men. It looked like a big night in Willcox.

Boone entered a sagging shed near the hotel and watched the wide street. He could see the lights of Lily Bell's beanery. A broad-shouldered man left the eating place and paused to light a cigar. The flare of the match revealed the broad face of Jim Dobie. The agent leaned against a post watching the street traffic. Boone left the shed and skirted the rear of the buildings and crossed the dimly lit street behind Dobie. 'Jim,' he called softly.

The agent whirled, dropping his hand to his Colt.

'It's Boone.'

'Get off the street!'

'Where can I see you?'

'There's an empty 'dobe at the west end of town. Go there.'

Boone faded into the darkness and found the adobe. In fifteen minutes Jim stepped into the darkness. 'What's up?'

'Eccles is out at Maxon's. Huerta was there and Eccles sent him down to Sonora. I don't know why.'

'How'd you get away?'

'Maxon left the ranch this morning. Eccles told me to follow him. Maxon is on a drunk in Dos Cabezas. I came here. I stopped by Eccles' adobe. Eli Bell was digging out there late this afternoon.'

Dobie spat. 'Most of the people of Willcox have been doing that ever since the holdup. You get a line on the express money?'

'No. What's been happening here?'

'Dowling has been drinking a lot ever since he heard Eccles got out of Yuma. Mean as hell. We've got to get this thing moving, Boone! I got a message from Mason. He wants action.'

'He'll just have to wait.'

'Supposing I go back to Maxon's with you and we run Eccles in?'

'We can't jump the gun now, Jim!'

'We're just not getting anywhere. I'd like to corral the whole bunch and beat the truth out of them.'

'Take it easy. Can you get me a pair of boots and a gunbelt?'

'Sure. What size boots?'

'Ten.'

'Same size as mine. I've got an old pair in my room. Your gunbelt is there too. Stay here.' Dobie left the building and vanished.

Boone rolled a smoke and sat down. Now and then he could hear the faint notes of the piano down the street.

Dobie returned and handed Boone a pair of mule-ear boots. Boone pulled on the old boots. 'Pretty worn,' he said.

'Best I could do.'

He handed Boone his gunbelt. Boone swung it about his waist. He took the six-gun from Dobie and slid it into the holster. 'Give me some cartridges.' Dobie handed him a box of forty-fours. Boone filled his belt loops.

Dobie peered out the window. 'Dowling saw me come out of the hotel. You'd better raise some dust out of here.'

'If we move I'll get a message to you somehow but stay away from the Maxon place.'

'All right.' The agent left the adobe.

Boone was at the corner when he heard feet grate on the hard earth. A big white hat showed through the darkness. Boone stepped into a doorway. His back bumped the door. *Quien es?* someone called loudly from within the house. Boone cursed under his breath. The man in the street was Bob Dowling.

'*Quien es?*' The door was pulled open, flooding Boone with lamp light. He darted around the corner and pounded up the alleyway. Dowling yelled. Then the quiet was shattered by the roar of a gun. Boone threw himself over a fence and ran across a stableyard. He ducked into the stable as Dowling came to a halt behind the fence.

'Spread out!' yelled Dowling. 'I seen Boone Shattuck!'

Boone eased open the front door of the stable and ran across the street just as two men rounded a corner. 'There he goes! Hey, Dowling!'

Boone raced past one of the hurdy-gurdy houses, jumped into a doorway. He heard Dobie's voice. 'He's headin' east!' The Wells-Fargo man was trying to lead Boone's pursuers off the track.

Boone flattened himself against the door. It gave a little. Boone eased open the door and stepped into a dim hallway. He could hear the excited voices of women at the front of the house.

'He musta gone in one of these places,' said Dowling from the alley.

Boone reached for the handle of the nearest door and pushed it open. A slim girl whirled. It was Nelly, the girl he had saved from Bob Dowling. 'What the hell!'

'Shut up,' said Boone. He closed the door. 'They're after me.'

'Who?'

'Dowling and some others.'

'I heard you broke outa Yuma.'

'Can I hide here?'

She pulled back a calico curtain. 'In there.'

Boone stepped into the closet in among dresses heavy with the odors of cheap perfume. Nelly dropped the hanging. 'What'd you do this time?' she asked.

'Nothing. I came into town to get something.'

'You damned fool!'

Boots thudded in the hallway. The door banged open. 'Yuh see a man come by here, Nelly?' It was Dowling.

'I don't let *any* man come by here, Bob.'

'Don't get funny!'

'I'm not. I haven't seen anyone.'

Boone peered between the hangings. Men were calling to each other out in the alley and in front of the hurdy-gurdy house.

Dowling waved his six-shooter. 'It was that bastard Shattuck. I'm sure.'

'Then keep lookin',' she said.

Dowling looked about the shabby room. 'Tell me if yuh see him.' He closed the door behind him.

Nelly turned. 'Wait until they move on.' She came to the hangings.'

'Dowling been giving you a hard time?'

She touched a pale bruise on her face. 'Yes. Some day I'll fix him.'

140

Boone could hear the men talking as they moved away. He stepped out into the room. 'I'll be on my way.'

She gripped his arm. 'You can stay. I'll lock the door. Won't nobody come in. They'll think I got a customer in here.'

He grinned. 'With those bloodhounds looking for me? No thanks.'

She flushed. 'Take me with you.'

'On the run? Hell no! I've got to make the border.'

'You got money?'

'Enough.'

She came close. 'Look. I got two hundred hidden. I can ride. Take me with you.'

He cupped her chin in his left hand and kissed her. 'No. They'll try to hunt me down.'

'You could send for me.'

'Maybe.'

'Will you?'

He had to get out of there.

She spoke swiftly. 'You send a message to Lily Bell and let me know where you are. I'll come.'

'All right. All right.'

She gripped him. 'You will, won't you?'

'Yes! Yes!'

She opened the door and looked up and down the hallway. 'Go ahead. It's clear.'

Boone passed her. She touched his face. 'You won't forget me, Boone?'

'No.' Boone walked to the rear door, eased it open and stepped into the filthy alley. Something bulked in the shadows across the alley. Boone started to run. Dowling jumped out and swung a length of wood at Boone. It struck him on the left shoulder. He gasped in pain and raised his Colt. The board hit him across the head and he went down on his knees, grunting in pain.

'You bastard,' Dowling said. 'I knowed you was in there.'

Dowling's foot came up. The spur slashed Boone's forehead. Blood dripped into his eyes, half-blinding him.

The door opened. Nelly screamed as she saw Boone's bloody face in the moonlight. Dowling cursed. 'Get in there, you fool!' he yelled. 'I'll settle you later!'

Her right hand came up, spit flame and smoke. Dowling gripped his belly. The board clattered to the ground. The double-barreled derringer spat again. Dowling went down as the second slug smashed into him. Nelly threw the gun at the fallen man. 'I did it for you!' she screamed at Boone.

Boone got up and picked up his Colt. A big man rounded the corner. It was Eli Bell, Colt in hand. 'What the hell is this?' he yelled. He saw Boone. 'You!'

Boone ran down the alley. Bell fired as Boone turned the corner. A horse was tied to a rack at the front of the house. Boone ripped the reins loose.

'Stop!' yelled Bell.

Boone swung up. He fired twice over Bell's head and lashed the excited horse. A gun spat behind him and the slug sang thinly over his head. Then he was on the open road, riding out.

A mile from town Boone slid from the horse and slapped him on the rump. The horse hammered west on the road. Two hundred yards from the road, Boone heard the pounding of hooves. Four men raced past, pursuing the riderless horse.

Boone sheathed the Colt and wiped the blood from his face with his bandanna. As he slogged on to where he had hidden the buckskin he thought of the screaming girl in the filthy alley with the smoking gun in her hand.

There was a sickness in Boone as he reached the buckskin.

CHAPTER TWELVE

Boone drew rein just outside of Dos Cabezas. The moon tinted the buildings a soft silver. A dog howled somewhere at the far end of town. Boone led the tired buckskin up the one street. A buckboard was outside the only saloon. Boone dropped the buckskin's reins and stepped up on the sidewalk beneath the shaggy ramada.

The bartender was mopping behind the zinctopped bar. One man stood at the bar. Another man sprawled across a table, his thin face in the liquor slops. It was Jonce Maxon, on a high lonesome.

Boone walked in. The bartender turned. 'Rye,' said Boone. He gripped the bottle that was slid toward him and filled his glass. Boone looked at Jonce. 'Well, hellsfire! It's Old Jonce Maxon!'

The barkeep nodded sourly. 'Drunk as a coot. Owes me for half a dozen rounds.'

Boone downed his drink. He walked to Maxon and pulled him from the chair. 'Come on, Jonce,' he said. 'I'm heading your way. I'll take you home.'

Jonce opened bleary eyes. His sour breath made Boone turn away. 'I gotta have another drink.'

'You've got a skinful.'

'One more.'

The bartender spat. 'He's like a gelding seeing a mare; it's all in his head.'

Jonce staggered toward the bar. Boone gripped the soiled shirt. 'Forget it, Jonce. Let's go home.'

Jonce turned slowly. 'I'm stayin' until the last dog is hung,' he announced.

The man at the end of the bar turned and

eyed Boone. 'Looks like they didn't hang *one* dog anyways.'

Boone turned away. The man knew him from somewhere. 'Come on, Jonce,' said Boone. The rancher whirled and drove a fist at Boone. It knocked off Boone's battered hat. The man at the bar eyed Boone and turned pale. Boone swung from the hip. The rancher went down like a falling pine. Boone slapped on his hat and carried the lean man to the door.

'He's got a tab here!' yelled the barkeep.

Boone dumped Jonce into the back of the buckboard. He walked back into the bar.

'It's him, I tell yuh!' the man at the bar was saying. 'The man who killed Billy Steen. I...'

'What does he owe?' asked Boone quietly.

'Ten drinks.'

'You said half a dozen before.'

'All right. All right.'

'I'm broke,' said Boone. He reached for the old Colt in his belt.

The barkeep reached under the bar. 'I got a scattergun here,' he warned.

Boone grinned. 'This Colt is old but it's worth half a dozen drinks. O.K.?'

'Yeh,' said the barkeep sourly.

Boone placed it on the bar and walked out. 'It's him,' the man insisted. 'Yuh better get holt of Sheriff Kelly.'

Boone tied the buckskin's reins to the

buckboard and climbed in. He slapped the reins down and drove swiftly out of the little town.

Jonce groaned. 'Who hit me?'

'You fell.'

'Christ! I *must* be drunk.'

'You are, Brother Maxon, you sure as hell are.'

The ranch house was dark when Boone drove the buckboard through the gate. He stopped in front of the house and helped Jonce to the ground. Boone unhitched the mules and turned them into the corral. The lights were on now in the old adobe. Boone unsaddled his horse and walked down into the hollow. He could hear voices as he neared the house. Two horses stood hipshot at the rear of the house. Boone sidled up to a window and looked in.

Bass Eccles sat at the far side of the table. Two men sat at opposite ends. One was thin of face, with a Mexican dandy mustache. His black hat was shoved back from his black curly hair. The other man was short and squat with a battered Mex sombrero pulled low over his stupid face, and the *barbiquejo* drawn taut under his fat jowls. He looked stolidly from the dark man to Bass Eccles and then back again.

'Like I said, boys. I had to leave Yuma in a hurry so there wasn't much time to let you know where I was,' Bass said.

The dark man spoke. 'We knew Huerta was heading west, Bass. Sim here gets the idea Bartolome was going to meet you. Looks like he was right for once.'

'I ain't that stupid,' said Sim.

Eccles' dark eyes saw Boone. An almost infinitesimal look of relief crossed the crafty face of the outlaw. 'Now, Dance,' said Bass to the dark man. 'You knowed I wasn't pullin' anythin' on yuh.'

'Just listen to him!'Younger said. 'Sweet as honey, ain't he?'

Sim leaned toward Bass. 'We want our sugar, Bass. Yuh know damned well I can't show my face around here. I need *dinero*. Pronto!'

'You'll get your share.'

'We want ten thousand apiece,' said Younger.

Bass downed his drink. 'Why, hellsfire, old Bass will give it to yuh.'

'When will Huerta be back?' asked Sim.

Bass grinned. 'I know what you're thinkin', Sim.'

Sim wet thick lips. 'Why split with the Mex? We can take his share and split three ways from the ace.'

'I swear to God you two *hombres* is crooks.'

'Listen to him,' jeered Younger. He slapped a gloved hand down on the table. 'Give out, Bass. Where's the sugar?'

'I'll get it.'

'Get it now,' said Sim. He drew his Colt and laid it on the table. His little eyes never left Eccles' face.

'All right. All right. I swear to God you fellas think I'm tryin' to do you outa it.'

'*Well?*' asked Younger.

Sim nodded. 'Gawd but we was taken in, Dance. This two-faced skunk gets the loot in his hands, gives us a few coins and then rushes us into Willcox. For an alibi, he says. We all get likkered up and never did see the rest of the loot.'

Bass shook his head. 'Yeh. If you had taken your share where would yuh be now? Six feet under with your tacks drove in tight. Younger here goes into Benson and flashes mint coins on a high lonesome. It's a wonder they didn't string him up.'

Dance stood up. 'All right. So I was likkered up! You got the *dinero*. Get it! Now!'

Bass waved a hand. 'I'll get it. Alone.'

'You will like hell,' said Sim.

Bass grinned lopsidedly. 'I should show you where *my* share is? I ain't that simple.'

Dance looked at Sim. 'Let him go. He won't get far.'

'I don't like it.'

Dance grinned. 'Leave them cutters here, Bass.'

'Sure. Sure.' Bass drew the Colts and placed them on the table.

Dance took out a hunting case watch and

148

snapped the lid open. 'Ten minutes. No more. You don't come back and we come lookin' for you.'

'Fair enough.' Bass grinned and left the house. He motioned to Boone. 'Stay near the door,' he whispered.

'What's your game?'

'Watch and follow my hand.'

Boone nodded. He watched Bass walk past the barn. He wanted to follow him but he could hear the soft jingle of spurs in the house and low talking.

Bass rounded the corner of the house carrying a ticking sack and went into the house. He left the door ajar. Boone eyed the three outlaws through the opening. Bass raised the heavy sack. 'Here yuh are, boys.'

'There ain't no twenty thousand in there,' said Dance.

'I didn't say there was. I'll get the rest after you look at this.'

Bass reached into his vest pocket and threw a handful of goldpieces on the table. They scattered and Sim dropped to his knees to pick up those that had rolled from the table, but Dance's eyes never left Bass. 'Let's see the rest,' he said.

'Sure.' Bass thrust a hand into the sack. He withdrew it swiftly, gripping a double-barreled derringer. It spat fire. Dance whirled away, cursing as he drew his Colt. Bass jumped back toward the door. Sim stood up.

Boone jerked the door open with his left hand. Dance turned and fired. The slug rapped into the thick adobe. Boone fired twice from the hip. Dance fell heavily. Boone jumped into the room and swung the Colt hard. It struck Bellam alongside the skull. He fell over his *amigo*.

Eccles was crouched in the corner, eyes wide and full of fear. 'It's all over, Bass,' said Boone.

Bass nodded. He stood up and placed the ticking bag on the table. 'Thought they had me,' he blustered.

Bass picked up Sim's Colt and aimed it at Bellam. Boone gripped Bass's wrist. 'Enough,' he said.

There was cold fury in Eccles' eyes. 'Yuh just killed Younger, didn't yuh?'

'He had a gun. He was on his feet. It was him or me. This is different.'

Boone took a length of rope and bound Bellam. He dragged the heavy man into the next room. 'We'd better get rid of Younger,' he said quietly.

Bass picked up the bottle and drank deeply, handed it to Boone. 'There's ten thousand of the haul,' he said.

'Where's the rest?'

Bass grinned.

'What's my split?'

'We'll talk about it later.' Bass slid his Colts into their sheaths. 'Thought yuh once said yuh was just average with a six-gun.'

'I had the edge,' said Boone. 'He didn't expect me.'

'That ain't the gun I gave yuh at the Kofas.'

Boone shook his head. 'I got this in Willcox along with the gunbelt and boots.'

'Yuh loco fool! I told yuh to stay outa town.'

'I trailed Maxon near there and lost him. I sneaked into town to look around. Found a drunk lying in an alley and took his gun belt and gun along with his boots.'

'Did yuh find Maxon?'

'He wasn't there. I found him in Dos Cabezas on a high lonesome and brought him back.'

'Anyone see you?'

'There was a shooting in Willcox. Bob Dowling saw me. In the shooting he was killed. I didn't do it.'

Eccles paled. 'Then they'll be after you. Why'd yuh come here?'

Boone grinned. 'For my share. I've gone through a lot of hell with you, Bass. I'm not pulling out now.'

Eccles wet his lips. 'Then we'll have to pull leather. Let's get rid of Younger.'

Boone got a spade from the barn. They dragged Younger out into the desert and buried him swiftly in the loose soil. When Eccles had once turned away Boone took Younger's wallet from his coat pocket and slid it into his own. Score one for Perry Thorne.

A shadow moved next to the adobe as they approached it. 'See who it is,' Bass said tensely.

The shadow moved. Marion Maxon came toward him. 'The shooting,' she said. 'What was it?'

Boone took her by the arm. 'Two men. Dance Younger and Sim Bellam. Dance was killed. Bellam is in there.'

She looked up at him. 'I thought it was you.'

'Would it matter?'

'Yes.'

Boone glanced back at Eccles. 'I think he wants to pull out,' he said softly. 'How's your father?'

'Dead to the world. I don't know how he got back.'

'I brought him from Dos Cabezas.'

Eccles came up to them. 'Tell your father to get ready to leave,' he said.

'He's staying here!'

'The hell he is. Neither are you. Get ready to move.'

Boone turned. 'Why?'

Eccles looked like a hungry lobo in the moonlight. 'I ain't leavin' anyone behind as can talk.'

'Where are we going?'

'Sonora. Pronto!'

Boone shook his head. 'Leave them alone. They won't talk.'

Bass rested his hands on his Colts. 'We can leave them at the border. Fair enough?'

'All right,' said Boone.

'Get our horses ready. Get rid of Younger's saddle and turn the hoss loose. We'll take Bellam along.'

Bass went into the house.

Boone gripped Marion by the shoulders. 'Listen,' he said. 'I'm a Wells-Fargo agent assigned to the express robbery case. I've got to play along with Bass for a time.'

'You lie!'

Boone took out his papers and his badge. 'See for yourself.'

She glanced at his credentials. 'How do I know this is true?'

'You've heard of Perry Thorne?'

'The man who was murdered in the express car? Yes.'

'He was my brother-in-law and my best friend. My sister died of a broken heart. They say it can't be done but it happened to her. Now do you believe me?' His face was harsh in the moonlight.

Suddenly she placed her arms about his neck. Boone kissed her. She clung to him. He kissed her again.

'Make black coffee. Sober Jonce up as quickly as you can. Do you have a gun?'

'Yes.'

'Bring it with you.'

Boone swiftly saddled the horses and led them outside. Eccles came over carrying three ticking sacks.

Boone went to the adobe and picked up his few articles. He picked up Eccles' Winchester and took it to the outlaw. They went into the ranch house. Jonce was seated at the table in his red undershirt swilling coffee from a granite cup. Marion was dressed in a split skirt and a fringed leather jacket. Eccles filled a sack with food and took it to the horses. Boone helped Jonce into shirt and coat. The rancher seemed to be in a daze. Boone helped him from the house.

'Where's Bellam?' asked Boone.

Eccles tightened his cinch. 'He won't be along,' he said.

'You can't leave him tied up like that,' said Boone.

Eccles grinned. 'He won't mind.'

Boone walked swiftly to the house. He stopped in the doorway of the second room. Sim Bellam lay on the floor. The heft of a knife protruded from his back. Boone closed the door and walked outside. Eccles had mounted and was holding the reins of Bellam's horse.

'You cold-gutted shark!'

'Get on your hoss,' Eccles said. 'He woulda done the same to me. *Vamonos!*'

They rode south on the rutted road. Boone

looked back at the deserted ranch buildings. Sim Bellam was dead from none of his doing. Score two for Perry Thorne. But the way of his death sickened Boone.

There were two left. The worst. Bass Eccles and Bartolome Huerta.

CHAPTER THIRTEEN

The moon was low down in the west when Bass Eccles drew rein and looked back. He stood up in his stirrups. Boone kneed the buckskin over to the outlaw. 'What's wrong?'

Eccles shrugged. 'Nothin' just had a feelin'.'

'What kind of feeling?'

'Like we was bein' followed.'

Boone looked north. Far behind them was a naked ridge. A lone horseman topped the ridge and rode slowly down into a hollow. Boone rolled a smoke. 'So?'

Eccles scowled. 'I don't trust no one.'

'I figured that,' said Boone dryly. He glanced at Bellam's horse, heavy laden with the ticking sacks. There was a chance he could drive off the pack horse. But Jonce Maxon was in bad shape, sagging in his saddle.

'Get offa the road,' Eccles said. 'Follow that

wash up ahead to the east. I'll come along.'

Boone rode up to Marion. 'Off the road,' he said.

He took Maxon's reins and led his horse into the wash. A quarter of a mile from the road he drew rein. An adobe perched on the lip of the wash with a faint road trending north and south from it.

Maxon shivered. Boone looked at the girl. 'Take him into that adobe. If we have time we can make coffee. Wrap him in a blanket.'

'Where are you going?'

'Back to the road.'

She looked toward the road. 'Be careful, Boone.'

'I'm safe enough.'

'While you were riding behind us he asked me if I had ever been in Mexico. He told me how beautiful it was.'

'So?'

'Before he went to prison he asked me to marry him. I refused. He told me he was rich and that he'd take care of my father.'

Boone laughed. *'Him?'*

'Maybe Dad and I could ride off now.'

'Your father wouldn't get far.'

'We can try.'

'No. Stick it out. I'm working for a slow-down. This may be it.'

She took Jonce into the abandoned adobe.

Boone slid from his horse and climbed the bank and circled away from the wash. He came out on the road a hundred yards from where he had left Bass Eccles. The outlaw was out of sight. A horse nickered from the brush.

The pack horse was tethered to a mesquite bush. Eccles was gone as though he had vanished from the earth. Boone drew out his knife and cut into one of the ticking sacks. He thrust his hand into the bag and touched stones. Swiftly he cut into the other two sacks. Stones.

Something grated behind Boone. He whirled. A gun flashed from the brush. The slug whipped along the side of Boone's skull. The earth and sky whirled as he went down. The gun flashed again. The slug picked at Boone's jacket. He rolled over and over into a hollow. Boots thudded against the hard earth.

Boone painfully drew his hide-out gun. A shadow formed in the brush. He fired twice. He heard Eccles curse. Boone crawled deep into the brush, ripping the cloth and skin from his knees. He was sure he was going under. Eccles crashed through the brush, fired twice. Boone jerked as a bullet slashed across his left bicep. Blood ran down his arm and dropped from his fingertips as he crawled into a low overhanging bank, pressing himself as far into it as he could.

There was no sound other than the wind. Then something grated not ten feet from

Boone. A tall shadow fell on the earth. Eccles passed by not ten feet away with cocked Colts in both hands. He stopped and looked about and then his face changed into an expression of deep-seated fear. He scuttled through the brush and ran off.

Boone closed his eyes. It was as though a powerful drug had been pumped into his system. Lethargy took over and then he knew no more.

The sun was warm on Boone's face as he opened his eyes. A sharp twinge of pain shot through his skull. His throat felt as though a dry hand was constricting it.

Boone rolled out onto the ground and winced as his wounded arm hit the hard earth. His left hand was caked with blood. He touched the side of his head. It had been a damned near thing.

Boone sat up and bowed his head in pain. Then he got to his feet, staggering a little as he tried to get his bearings. The sun was well up. He walked up to the lip of the hollow. He could see the adobe to the east. Slowly he approached the building. He walked to the doorway and pushed aside the sagging door. The big room he looked into was empty of life.

Boone walked in and leaned against the wall. A terrible thirst gripped him. Boone walked out the back door and looked down into the wash. The floor of the wash was trampled with the marks of many hoofs. The trail led up the bank of the wash and off into the thick brush.

He rolled a smoke and lay on the floor smoking slowly until he felt better.

Eccles had turned on him like the lobo he was. But who had been the lone horseman on the road behind them? Then it came to Boone. Bartolome Huerta, possibly. Eccles had fixed Boone's clock. Then the thought of Marion in Eccles' hands hit Boone like a blow. He forgot about the gold and Perry Thorne. He stood up and put on his hat and then slogged toward the road under the beating sun.

It was late afternoon when Boone saw the adobe set back from the road. A bearded man came out of the building and looked curiously at him as he staggered toward the adobe. He raised a rifle. 'What do you want?' he asked.

Boone raised his hands. 'I've been shot,' he said.

The man came forward. 'God,' he said. 'You look like a haunt.'

'I was held up,' he said.

'Come on into the house.'

Boone followed the man into the house and sat down in a chair. The man eyed him. 'I'm Warren Byles,' he said. 'Prospector. Let me take a look at them wounds.'

Boone closed his eyes as Byles removed the bandages. 'Clean,' he said. 'When did this happen?'

'Last night about five miles from here.'

'So? Who did it?'

'Bandit.'

Warren got a pan and bathed the wounds and then treated them. He bandaged them neatly. 'Useta be a medical orderly at Fort Bowie,' he said. 'Do a good job if I say so myself.'

'Thanks.'

'I'll get some chuck. Start you with coffee.'

Boone sipped the hot liquid. Warren busied himself at the fireplace. 'Got some sonofagun stew left over from last night. Fair enough?'

'Anything will do, Byles.'

The prospector set out the food and watched Boone eat. 'Funny thing last night,' he said. 'Four people come by, riding like hell. Couldn't sleep. I heard the horses coming and walked outside. One of them bastards took a shot at me.'

'What'd they look like?'

'One was a young woman. Real tall hombre. Shorter man, looked like a Mex. Another man, hanging onto his saddle-horn. They had a packhorse with them carrying some sacks.'

Boone stopped eating. 'Sacks?'

'Yeh. Ticking sacks. The tall mean-looking bastard was the one that shot at me. I

160

wonder why?'

'Guess they didn't want you to get a good look at them.'

'Funny thing. I was sure I knew the hombre that shot at me.'

'Bass Eccles.'

Byles paled. 'My God! That was him all right!'

'You know him?'

'Hell yes!' Byles smashed a fist into his palm. 'I knew him in Tombstone. I was working for Wells-Fargo then, as bullion guard. I never trusted him when he rode along even if he was deputy-sheriff.'

Boone eyed the bearded man. 'Wells-Fargo?'

'Yeh. Damned good job.'

Boone slid a hand into his pocket and took out his credentials. Byles' eyes widened as he saw the badge. 'By God! You after Eccles?'

Boone nodded.

Byles got a bottle from a cupboard. 'I thought Bass was in Yuma.'

'He was.'

'They ever pin that express train robbery on him?'

'He engineered it.'

'I'll bet he did.' Byles filled two cups.

'Last night he turned on me near that old adobe beside the wash and shot me down.'

'That's like him.'

'Byles, will you go back there with me?'

'Why?'

'I want to look around.'

'Keno. I'll get my horse and my pack mule. You can take the horse.' Boone refilled his glass.

Byles led the horse and mule up to the front of the adobe and slid his rifle into its sheath. Boone weaved a little as he walked out to the horse. They rode north.

Byles led the way off the road into the thick brush to the old adobe. A hundred yards from the house he found three mounded heaps of stones. He knew they came from the ticking sacks, yet Byles had said the pack horse had been heavily laden with ticking sacks. Behind the rock knoll he found a place where the soil had been disturbed. Byles looked at him. 'See if you can find something to dig with,' said Boone.

'There's an old spade in the brush.'

Five feet down Byles struck wood. He threw out several pieces of thick wood covered with reddish wax. He pulled a small tin box from the hole. He handed it to Boone. Boone pried it open with the spade. A battered dollar watch was in it. It suddenly dawned on Boone that the outlaw's perverted sense of humor had planted a horse on whoever would dig in the emptied cache.

Byles wiped the sweat from his face. 'Well?'

Boone squatted. 'The gold was here.

There's no doubt about that. The sacks Bass brought here were full of those stones. He emptied them and filled the sacks with the loot. Forty thousand worth, Warren.'

'Chihuahua! And I've been living within five miles of a fortune all this time.'

Boone swayed a little.

'We'd better get back to my place.'

Back at Byles' adobe Boone lay down on the cot. Byles shook his head. 'You should have rested,' he said. 'You look gaunt as a gutted snowbird.'

'I feel like it. Byles, will you do something for me? Wells-Fargo business?'

'Sure.'

'Take a message to Willcox. To a man named Jim Dobie. He's another Wells-Fargo detective. Get him back here as fast as you can.'

'Certainly!'

'There's a lot of reward money out for Eccles. You'll get in on it.'

'I can use a new grubstake.'

'You'll get it.' Boone took paper and pencil from the table and wrote swiftly telling Dobie of what had happened. He looked up at Byles. 'I'll need your horse.'

Byles rubbed his jaw.

'You'll be taken care of.'

'Take what you need. Where will you be?'

Boone lay down again. 'Naco. If I leave there I'll leave a message with the *alcalde*.'

Byles took the message. 'I'll ride my mule. You ain't in any shape to travel, Shattuck.'

Boone looked up at the prospector. 'I'll follow Bass Eccles clear to Nicaragua if I have to.'

Byles looked at the drawn face, with the long scar accentuated against the pale skin. But it was the cold blue eyes that told him further talk was useless.

CHAPTER FOURTEEN

The shadows were deep in the twisted streets of Bisbee when Boone tethered Warren Byles' sorrel to a rail half a block from the lamplit Wells-Fargo office. He plodded wearily toward the light. His head still ached and his left arm was stiff.

Boone stopped on the boardwalk in front of the office. A thin man was seated at a desk, his face shaded by a green eyeshade. Boone opened the door and walked in. The man looked up quickly and dropped his right hand below the desk. 'Can I help you?' he asked. He glanced at the wall clock. 'It's almost closing time,' he added uncertainly.

'You the Wells-Fargo agent?'

The man grinned. 'I wouldn't be sitting here going over these damned reports if I

164

wasn't, would I?'

'I'm Boone Shattuck. You alone?'

'Yes.'

Boone slid his hand into his coat. The agent raised his head quickly. 'There's nothing here,' he said.

'I was working with Jim Dobie up in Willcox. I'm after Bass Eccles.'

'Bass Eccles? He's in Yuma.'

'He got out last week.'

The agent leaned back in his chair. 'Where's your credentials?'

Boone placed them on the desk. The agent nodded. 'I'm Charley Corson. You must be all right. You wouldn't know about Jim Dobie if you weren't. What's your problem?'

'I need money and information.'

'I can give you money. What do you want to know? Why did you come here?'

'Where else would Eccles and Huerta go? He's in Mexico by now.'

Corson stood up and pulled down the shade. 'You figure on following them?'

'Yes.'

Corson eyed Boone. 'Last year one of our agents, Danny Crook, followed Bartolome Huerta down into the Rio de Bavispe country. He didn't come back.'

Corson felt an icy finger trace the length of his spine as he looked at the man facing him. The room suddenly seemed cold despite the warmth of the night. Corson looked away.

'Eccles has friends in Sonora. You'd be spotted.'

'My beard is growing. It'll hide this scar.'

Corson was about to say that nothing would hide those eyes but he thought better of it. This was a different man than Danny Crook who had been purely after the reward money. There was some primal urge driving this strange man on into Sonora after two of the toughest men in the border country. 'I said Eccles had friends, Shattuck.'

'He also has enemies. A man like Eccles always has enemies.'

Corson shrugged. 'There is a man in Naco. Hilario Chavez. He always has information to sell. He has no love for Bartolome Huerta. You can find him in the Cantina of the Doves almost any night. He's cagey.'

'I'll find him.'

Corson placed his papers in a file. 'What else do you need?'

'A rifle. Winchester .44/40. A good saddle and a good horse. Money for clothes and some supplies. A place to sleep.'

'You want me to get the stuff?'

'I'll get it. You give me the *dinero*.'

Corson opened a cash drawer. 'How much?'

'Five hundred will do.'

Corson counted out the bills. He locked the drawer. 'Get a room at the St Elmo. They don't ask questions there. I'll nose

166

around town tonight. Look for me about midnight.'

Boone left the office. Corson watched him from the open door, shook his head and then locked up for the night.

Boone entered a general store. He bought a good used Colt Peacemaker and a Winchester. As an afterthought he also purchased a Remington double-barreled, over-and-under derringer and a box of .41 caliber cartridges for it. He completed his purchases with some tinned food, flour, tobacco and a canteen. He led the sorrel to a livery stable and then went to the shabby St Elmo where he got a room.

He was asleep when Corson tapped at the door. The agent dropped into a chair and opened a bottle. He filled glasses and lit up a stogie. 'Huerta was seen here in town some days ago. Heading south. Later he was seen again, heading north. No one has seen Eccles. A teamster told me he saw four people riding south, east of town, a day or so ago. A tall thin man, obviously sick. Another tall man, dark-faced. A Mex. A young woman. In a helluva hurry.'

Boone nodded. 'Eccles and Huerta. The sick man was Jonce Maxon. The woman, his daughter Marion.'

Corson studied Boone. 'Why are Maxon and his daughter with Eccles?'

Boone sipped his drink. 'Eccles was afraid

Maxon would talk.'

'It would be like Eccles to kill him to keep his mouth shut.'

Boone looked up. 'Eccles is making a play for the girl.'

'So?' Corson downed his drink. 'Seems to me you've got more than company interest in this deal, Shattuck.'

'I may have.' His eyes grew dark.

'Take it easy. I've located a good horse for you. Jimmy Logan, at the livery stable will let you see it tomorrow. I've got a good Frazier hull you can use. I'll tell Jimmy to let you have it.'

'*Gracias.*'

Corson stood up and reached for the bottle. 'Leave it here,' said Boone.

Corson withdrew his hand. 'Get some sleep,' he said. 'You need it.'

Boone nodded. The agent left the room. Boone downed two quick slugs and dropped on the bed. His hand traced the bruised area on the side of his head.

CHAPTER FIFTEEN

Boone slowly rode the bayo coyote gelding through the wide dusty streets of Naco, lined with shabby one-story adobes and *jacals*. Faded signs advertising merchandise, liquors and beers, were sprawled across the fronts of some of them. The *ranchita,* a noisome area of brothels and saloons, was full of life. Pianos tinkled offkey. A guitar strummed from one of them. A ragged parrot squawked from a cage hanging in front of one of the cantinas. A crude painting of a dove showed on the facade of the building. Boone tethered his horse.

Boone's spurs jingled as he walked into the dimly lit cantina and sat down at a rickety table. A girl, hardly more than sixteen, swayed up to him, wiggling her full hips, letting her *camisa* drop from a smooth brown shoulder. Boone shook his head and ordered *aguardiente* from the waiter. He eyed the men in the place as he drank. A night's sleep had done him good. Corson had sent a message to Hilario Chavez that morning.

A little man sat at a table ten feet from Boone, idly picking at a battered guitar. His liquid eyes lifted and looked at Boone, then he stood up and walked to Boone's table. 'Perhaps the senor would like a *cancione?*' he asked in his native tongue

Boone nodded. The little man softly played and sang La Raza de Bronce Que Sabe Morir. The Bronze Race That Knows How to Die. The Mexican tribute to the Yaquis and Tarahumares. Boone nodded and tossed him a coin. He shoved the bottle toward the little man, who filled a glass. 'You are Senor Shattuck?'

'Yes.'

'You are visiting Sonora?'

'In a way.'

'Hunting?'

'Perhaps.'

'It is not a good hunting season ... for game.'

'I do not hunt game, Hilario.'

'So? That is odd. Is it women you hunt? Gold? Silver? Perhaps the Lost Tayopa Mine?'

'None of those.'

'Anastacio Madera has a fine chart showing the way to El Naranjal, the fabulous lost mine. I can get it for you for a few pesos.'

'No.'

Hilario filled his glass. He looked about the dim cantina. 'Perhaps you seek Bass Eccles and Baratolome Huerta?'

'Perhaps.'

'Good!' Hilario sipped his liquor.

'Huerta is perhaps a friend of yours, Hilario?'

'That *bazofa?* Mother of God!'

Boone rolled a smoke. 'Where are they?'

'Who knows?'

'You have not seen them?'

'Not I. But they have been through here.'

'So? Where did they go?'

'Of that I am not sure. It is said they went to Tres Jacales.'

'Where is that?'

'Near the Rio Magdelena not far from Pitiquito.'

'Is it far?'

'Yes. Many leagues.'

'You are sure?'

Hilario nodded.

'How do you know?'

'My brother Jesus is a Rurale under Colonel Kosterlitzky. He told me.'

'How do I get there?'

'It is dangerous. They are hard men. They have many friends. Outlaws.'

'I will go.'

Hilario eyed the cold-eyed gringo sitting across from him. 'Why do you go?'

'I want Bass Eccles.'

'And not Huerta?'

'Yes.'

'To kill them?'

'Perhaps.'

Hilario smiled. 'Good.'

171

'Why do you hate them, Hilario?'

Hilario plucked at his guitar. 'I had a sister once. A child. Pretty as the mountain flowers growing beside the rushing streams. She was my pet, you understand, for my father and mother were killed by the Yaquis. For a time I rode with Augustin Chacon, the great bandit. Huerta was one of us. I was but a young man. There was a time when the Rurales chased us. We separated. Huerta and I fled into the Sierra Madre to my village where we were safe. Or so I thought. Huerta saw my sister. I watched him like an eagle. Then one night I went down the mountain to see if the Rurales were about. I was caught. Someone had informed on me. For a time I was in the prison at Hermosillo. When I was released I came home.' Hilario stopped talking and refilled his glass. He tossed it down.

'So?'

The Mexican leaned forward. 'Huerta had taken my sister. A child. She died in Nacozari from a beating he gave her.'

'Why did you not kill him?'

Chavez spread out his thin brown hands, palms upwards. 'I was no longer one of Chacon's men. The Rurales watched me. Huerta had many friends in the mountains. So I came here. The Rurales pay me for information. Your officers do likewise. It is a good life. Dangerous, but easy. I wait for a chance at Huerta. I am patient. I say to my-

172

self: Hilario, some day a man will come who will look for Bartolome Huerta. He will want to kill him. I will help that man. You are that man.'

Boone rolled another cigarette and handed it to the Mexican. Then he rolled another for himself. 'You will tell me the way to Tres Jacales?'

'It is a hard road. Past Cananea to the headwaters of the Rio Magdelena. Thence to Imuris, Magdelena, Santa Ana, by a fair road. Then westerly to Altar and then Pitiquito.'

Boone nodded. 'What do I owe you?'

Hilario looked hurt. 'You will pay me when Bartolome Huerta dies beneath those guns you carry. For favor, Mister Shattuck, let him die slowly, and tell him about Hilario Chavez, so that he knows I helped you. For favor?'

'Yes. For favor.'

'Good!' Hilario took another drink. 'Then perhaps we will meet again?'

'Let us hope so.'

'Go with God!'

'Go with God, Hilario.' Boone watched the little man leave the cantina. He finished his drink, paid his tab, and left.

CHAPTER SIXTEEN

Boone squatted in the shade of his horse, a cigarette pasted to his lower lip, eyeing the thread of dust which rose on the rough trail below him. His eyes never left the lone horseman riding steadily and directly toward the low mounded hills where Boone was waiting. Boone had traveled about a hundred miles in the four days since he had left Naco, seeing no one except occasional *paisanos* on the yellow roads. They had all told him he was on the road to Pitiquito, without a doubt.

The sun beat down on the parched earth, forming shimmering veils that hurt the eyes. A ragged buzzard soared on motionless pinions high above him. A *zopilote,* like a scrap of charred paper floating in the cloudless sky. Boone eyed the repulsive bird of carrion. He was waiting with spidery patience for something. Something or someone.

Boone stood up and led the horse into a hollow. He poured some of his water into the hollow of his hat and let the bay drink. His water was low. He allowed himself a sip and corked the canteen. Then he walked up the slope and dropped in the shade of a naked shaft of rock. The horseman was a mile away now. Boone slid the rifle forward and levered a round into the chamber.

The man was close enough for Boone to see he rode wearily. The dust threaded away from the hoofs and was raveled by the hot wind.

The man rounded a turn and looked up. Boone gripped his Winchester and then relaxed his grip. There was something familiar about the stocky figure. 'I'll be damned,' he said softly. 'Jim Dobie!' He stood up and waved his hat. Jim slid from the saddle, jerked his rifle from its sheath and slapped his gray on the rump. The gray trotted off into the brush. Dobie jumped into cover.

'Jim!' yelled Boone. 'It's me! Shattuck!'

Dobie came slowly out of the brush and plodded up the trail followed by the tired gray. 'God,' he said. 'I'm parched!'

Boone walked to his bay, got the canteen and handed it to Dobie. Dobie looked at the horse. 'All right?'

Boone nodded. Dobie watered the gray. 'Where's the next water?'

'*Quien sabe?* Pitiquito can't be far away.'

'*'Sta bueno!*' Dobie drank sparingly. He looked at Boone. 'I'm de-hydrated.'

Boone grinned, wincing as a lip cracked. 'You'll live.'

'You look chipper enough.'

'I'm part lizard.'

Dobie squatted in the shade and took out

a long nine. He lit it and watched the bluish tobacco smoke drift off. 'Hilario Chavez told me you had headed this way. I've been riding like hell.'

'Foolish in this country.'

'Maybeso. But I've come to take you back with me.'

'No go.'

Dobie's green eyes went hard. 'I wired Mason. He told me to stay out of Mexico and keep you out.'

'I'm here.'

'We'll go to Pitiquito and then head back.'

Boone lazily leaned back against the rock. 'You'll go back alone.'

Dobie withdrew the cigar from his mouth. 'You'll obey orders! There's hell to pay! We lost Danny Crook down here. The Guardia Rurale did nothing about it, claiming they should have been notified he was one of our operatives.'

'That would have saved him?'

Dobie shrugged. 'I doubt it. The fact is that the Mexican Government has no extradition deal with us even if we located Eccles.'

'Tough.'

Dobie closed his eyes. 'What do you expect to do when you find Eccles?'

'Kill him.'

'You will like hell!' Dobie threw away his cigar. 'We want him back in Arizona!'

'You've got a fat chance of getting him

there. He has the gold with him.'

'It's more than the gold! There were valuable papers in that express car. If you kill Eccles they'll be lost forever.'

Boone shrugged.

Dobie stood up. 'Let's get to Pitiquito.' He looked up at the sky. 'Filthy thing.'

'He's probably waiting for you, Jim.'

Dobie whirled. 'What do you mean?'

'You're not used to the desert. They seem to know. I didn't see him until you showed up.'

'You're loco with the heat!'

'Perhaps.' Boone picked up his rifle. 'Let's go. *Vamonos!*'

They rode to the west in the face of the hot sun. Now and then Boone looked at the agent. He was far gone with the heat and thirst.

They met the *paisano* in a bend of the trail. The old Mexican took off his great hat. 'Jorge Esteban, *servidor de ustedes,*' he said in the old phrasing.

Boone leaned on his saddlehorn. 'Greetings, friend,' he said. 'How many leagues to Pitiquito?'

'Not many. Perhaps an hour's ride.'

'Thank you.'

'It is nothing. Follow the trail.' The old man hesitated. He eyed them closely. 'It is not a good place at this time, sirs.'

'How so?'

'There are bandits there. There has been some killing. Mother of God! I fled from the town. I return to my barranca where I can be at peace with my goats.'

'Bandits?' asked Dobie.

'Yes. Yes. Some of the men of Chacon. The place is a veritable nest of eagles! Rape, killings, drunken revels. You must not go there. The Rurales are not within many leagues.'

Boone cursed. Dobie slowly wiped his red face. 'There is water nearby?'

'Yes. In the hills to the north. There is a fork in the trail a league from here. Turn right. Father Joseph is there at the little ruined mission. A good man. There is water there and shade.'

Boone tossed the old man a few coins. 'Thank you, friend.'

'Thank you. It is nothing.' The old man watched the two dusty gringos ride into the sun. '*Ay de mi*, Pablo,' he said to his shabby burro. 'These Americans are mad. To travel into the Gran Desierto at this time of year.'

The tumbled ruins had almost reverted to the earth from which they had been built. Boone drew rein on a rise and studied the little mission. A thread of smoke arose from the far side of the ruins. A pair of burros grazed on a patch of greenery near a pile of rocks. Dobie sagged in his saddle. 'If there isn't water here I'm done for.'

'Take it easy. Someone is there.' He spurred the flagging bay down the slope. The sound of the clashing hoofs brought a robed man to the front of the ruins. A padre. He shaded his eyes and watched them. Boone drew rein near him. 'Good day, Father,' he said politely. 'There is water?'

The padre nodded. 'Yes, my son. In the tanks there.'

Dobie slid from his horse and ran awkwardly across to the rocks. He dropped on his belly and began to drink.

The padre shook his head. 'He will be ill.'

'You are alone?' asked Boone.

'Yes. Some of my laborers have gone into Pitiquito for supplies. They will return tomorrow.'

'Some of Chacon's men are in Pitiquito.'

The padre held up his hands. 'Then there will be trouble!'

Boone led the bay to the water and let him drink a little. Dobie raised his red face and then suddenly rolled away from the rock pan to retch out the water he had taken in.

Boone sipped a double handful of water and went to the old padre. The man was sitting in the shade of a brush ramada watching the sun die in an agony of rose and gold to the west. 'Is it not beautiful?' he asked.

Boone squatted beside him. 'And deadly.'

'Yes. It is so. Where are you going, my son?'

'We are looking for three men and a woman.'

The padre eyed Boone. 'Three men and a woman came here some days ago. Two men and a woman left.'

'What do you mean?'

'Come.' The padre got stiffly to his feet and led Boone across a rise to a level space. The ground was mounded with desert rocks. A cemetery. A fresh mound was at one side surmounted by a crude cross. 'This man died here. There was nothing we could do. An American.'

'What was his name?'

'An odd one. Jonce Maxon.'

Boone took off his hat.

'You knew him?'

'Yes.'

'He is with God. He was suffering terribly.'

'The other three?'

The padre looked off to the north-west. 'They rode that way. They said they were going to Puerto Penasco. I rode after them to tell them it was the wrong trail. The tall American cursed me and told me to mind my own business. They went into the Gran Desierto. The Camino del Diablo.'

'The Devil's Road.'

'Yes. The trail followed by Padre Kino many years ago. A place of heat and thirst. Death is the only inhabitant.' The padre looked speculatively at Jim Dobie. 'The wings of death have brushed him close.'

They walked back to the abandoned mission. 'What do you do here, Father Joseph?' asked Boone.

The padre wiped his face. 'Many years ago this was a mission of the church as you can see. The Apaches and Yaquis raided it constantly. In time the people here were wiped out. The Franciscans abandoned it. An effort was made to rebuild it in 1822, but shortly after that time the Franciscans were expelled from Mexico, after Mexico won her independence from Spain. This place was forgotten. I received permission to dig into the ruins for relics of the past.'

'It is hard work?'

'Yes. Very hard. My men complain of the heat and the loneliness.'

They sat down under the Ramada. 'The woman who was with those two men, Father Joseph, how did she look?'

The padre made a pitying gesture with hands and head. 'Her eyes were dry when we buried her father. She asked for my help saying she was with those men against her will. Later, the American told me she was his sister and was not well in the head. I did not believe him but what could I do?'

Boone nodded. 'You do not know where they went?'

The padre shrugged. 'Into the Gran Desierto, as I said, possibly to reach the Colorado by the Smuggler's Trail. The trail leads from Quitovaquita, south of Ajo in your United States, thence north, thence west to Las Playas, thence northwest through Tinajas Altas, the High Tanks, to Yuma in Arizona Territory on the south side of the Gilas. It is in our records in the mission at Hermosillo that Father Kino used such a trail.'

'You have been on it?'

The Mexican nodded. 'Yes, as a much younger man. Our beasts died from lack of water. We almost died. Three of us made the Colorado.' The padre shook his gray head. 'A strange land, almost unreal, as though on the moon or a distant planet. There are voices there that speak to a man's inner soul and tell him strange terrible things. A man must put his trust in God out there or lose his reason. A man is alone, yet not lonely, for he is close to God in that terrible place. Do you believe in God, my son?'

'Yes, Father Joseph.'

'It is well. You will need him.'

'Do you think I will go out there?'

The old man smiled. 'Two gringos, as my people call you Americans, ride out of the desert, with ready weapons. They ask about those that have gone before, not with anxiety for loved ones, but with hate in their souls. You seemed sorry for the death of that man who died. The two men that were here were in great haste to bury him and move on. So it was obvious that *they* did not feel sorrow for him. When I told you of the frightened young woman it seemed as though Satan himself stared at me from those cold eyes of yours. Yes, you will follow them. There will be more violence.'

Jim Dobie lay in the shadow of the tanks, now and then raising his head and dropping it back. He was through.

Boone watched him. 'Tomorrow I will leave. My friend cannot go on. Can I leave him here?'

'Certainly.'

Boone nodded. 'I will pay you.'

The padre shook his head. 'I will accept nothing. A donation for the church perhaps, if you can afford it. For me ... nothing. He is one of God's children.'

Boone made a bed for Jim inside the old ruin. Boone helped him to the bed and lowered him. Dobie opened his eyes. 'This stops us, Boone.'

Boone leaned against the wall. 'You. Not me.'

'My orders were to bring you back.'

Boone laughed. 'You're lucky if you get back yourself, Jim.'

The sick man tried to get up. He was a company man, all right. Boone walked outside. The sun was gone and already the desert was cool. The old padre was preparing food.

'Let me help you.'

The old man smiled. 'No. It is a simple pleasure to cook a meal and serve you. Do not deny me, my son.'

Boone walked to the cemetery and looked down at the grave of Jonce Maxon. He placed a gayly striated stone on top of the pile of rocks, and returned to eat.

CHAPTER SEVENTEEN

The fire crackled in a corner of the ruined room, casting grotesque shadows on the walls. The night wind soughed about the ancient walls of the mission. Boone methodically checked the small keg Father Joseph had given him. It seemed sound enough. Before him, on a square of cloth, lay the dried fruits and meats which the old padre had traded to him for the last tins of food which he had brought from Naco. He glanced at Jim Dobie. The detective was asleep. It had been a close call for him.

Boone packed his food into his saddlebags. He carried the keg to the rock pan and filled it, letting it sink beneath the water to swell tight the seams. He had his two canteens and the one big one Dobie had brought along.

The padre was asleep on his pallet in the old sacristy. Boone passed softly through the dim room, faintly lit by the firelight from the next room. Boone examined the map that the padre had given him. The thing that puzzled him was why Bass Eccles had traveled west instead of south. The padre had known vaguely of a place called Tres Jacales, but, as he had said, it was a common enough name in Mexico.

Boone gathered his gear together. His saddlebags, guns, canteens and spare clothing. He eyed his boots and then looked at Dobie's. A spare pair of boots might be necessary. He pulled the boots toward him, slipped off his own and tried on Dobie's. They weren't a bad fit.

'What the hell do you think you're doing?'

Boone looked up. Jim was up on one elbow, eyeing his boots on Boone's feet. 'You won't need them for a time, Jim,' he said quietly.

'Damn you! You'll return with me to Bisbee!'

Boone pulled off Dobie's boots and put on his own, then leaned back against the wall. 'Maybe you don't remember what I said back in Willcox, Jim. I told you I was out to get the four men who did the job. Two of them are dead. There are two left.'

Dobie shifted his hand beneath his blanket. 'You've worked with the devil's luck!'

'I'm breaking the case, Jim. I went to Yuma to befriend Eccles, which I succeeded in doing. I helped force him into the open with

185

the stolen gold.'

'Yeh! Where is he now? Out in the desert heading for freedom!'

'He's trying to reach the coast, I'll swear. Something drove him west.'

Dobie rubbed his forehead. He was a damned sick man. 'Look, Boone. We can wire ahead to Yuma and San Diego for our men to be on the lookout for him.'

Boone shook his head.

Dobie lay back. 'You don't give a fiddler's damn about Wells-Fargo. This is a vengeance trail for you, Shattuck.'

'Marion Maxon is in his hands.'

Dobie raised his head. 'So that's it?'

'Yes.'

'What do you think has happened to her by now? In the hands of those two skunks?'

Boone stood up. 'I aim to find out.'

'You're loco! One man can't go after them.'

Boone eyed the sick man from lowered brows.

'Damn you! You're no longer a Texas Ranger!'

Boone shook his head. 'It's no use, Jim. Padre Joseph will take care of you. You'll be all right.'

Dobie flipped back his blanket. The firelight glinted on his cocked Colt.

Boone's Winchester leaned against the far wall. His Colts were in the corner on his bed. But beneath his left sleeve was the

Remington derringer, clipped to his wrist. 'You can't hold me here all night like this, Jim,' he said.

'I'll get the padre to tie you up.'

'I doubt it.'

There was a slight touch of madness in the tired green eyes. 'You called me a company man once. I am. Enough of a company man to obey the orders of Wells-Fargo, and to hell with the Texas Rangers.'

Boone suddenly shoved his left foot beneath his saddlebags, lifting them and throwing them at Dobie. Boone hit the floor as the Colt crashed, rolled over and jumped to his feet as Dobie tried to clear the heavy leather bags from about his head. Boone launched a kick that caught the detective behind the right ear. Dobie sagged down and dropped the Colt. Boone snatched it and looked up into the pale face of the padre. 'It is nothing, Father Joseph,' he said. 'The sun and thirst have made him slightly mad. He tried to stop me from leaving.'

The padre crossed himself. 'I do not understand. Perhaps the sun and thirst have made him mad. Yet there is a more terrifying madness in you. I am afraid for you, my son.'

Boone gathered his gear and weapons together and walked out into the moonlight. He saddled his bay and slung the saddlebags into place. He lashed the keg into place and slid his Winchester into its sheath. The old man came out behind him. Boone pressed some bills into his thin hands. 'For the church. You will take care of him?'

'Of course.'

'Goodbye then, Father Joseph.'

'Go with God, my son.'

Boone led the bay toward the faint trail which led over a rise. He glanced at the lonely cemetery as he passed. At the top of the rise he looked back. The padre, a strange hunched figure in black, had his head bowed as though praying.

Boone gigged his horse and rode down the slope in the moonlight.

CHAPTER EIGHTEEN

The desert was a moonlit sea, dappled by deep pools of shadow in the hollows. The mountains to Boone's right and behind him, were dim hulks in the distance. The sands were still warm beneath his feet. The wind sighed across the wastes, setting the mesquite, ocotillo and occasional yucca into swaying motion. There was no sign of man to be seen.

It was several hours before dawn when Boone stopped and tethered the bay to a stunted growth. He dropped on the ground and instantly fell asleep.

The false light of the first dawn showed in the eastern skies when Boone awoke. He swung up on the bay and rode northwest toward the mountains which showed faintly in the dawn light.

Noon found him crossing a rippled area where now and then a saguaro lifted its forked arms. His eyes picked out the trail winding up the slopes of a low range of hills miles ahead of him.

It was late afternoon when he was in among the sandhills. Higher and higher he went until suddenly the trail rounded a conical hill and he saw the *jacals* below him, already in the shadow of the hills to the west of them. Boone dropped the reins and walked forward to study the little settlement. There was no sign of life. A ghost town.

Boone led the tired bay down the twisting trail. He left the horse in a hollow and withdrew his Winchester from its sheath. He padded forward and then stopped short. Four of the buildings were of adobe. Two of fieldstone. But three of them were definitely *jacals*, formed of upright poles set into the hard earth and plastered with adobe. *Tres Jacales*.

Boone eased forward, keeping to the deep shadows, peering into each building as he passed. They were all empty. Beyond the last building lay a dead horse with bloated belly. The eyes and soft parts of the carcass had been torn by beaks and claws. The stench from the body closed about him as he passed it. On a low rise he saw an obelisk, cut from desert stone, with the once-sharp edges rounded and smoothed by the sand laden winds.

He came close to it and peered at the incised letters written in Spanish. 'The inhabitants of Tres Jacales killed by the Yaquis,' he translated. 'November 10th, 1881. Christians, for the sake of God, pray for their souls.'

Boone looked at the mounded graves beyond the obelisk. There were many. He leaned on his Winchester. There was an intense loneliness about the place. A brooding loneliness that seemed to reach out to engulf his soul.

The water was behind the town. Rock pans surrounded by humped rocks. The water was low but palatable. Boone went back for the bay.

The hollow was empty.

The hoof marks led off to the south. Boone trotted after the stray. He topped a rise which gave a clear view of miles of desert. The bay was not in sight, nor could he see any tracks on the rippled sands.

Boone bent forward and followed the tracks which showed faintly on the hard earth, windswept and barren. Then they vanished. A cold feeling came over him. He whirled swiftly.

There was no one there.

Boone climbed the low hills behind the town. He shook his head and walked down into the town. Then he heard the muffled stamp of a hoof in the largest of the buildings. He walked toward it, leaned his Winchester against the outer wall and walked in. The bay whinnied from the darkness. Something hard pressed against Boone's back. He jerked a little as something penetrated his skin and a trickle of blood worked down his back.

'*Gracias,* gringo,' someone said behind Boone.

Boone raised his hands. 'What do you want?'

'Mother of the Devil! It is you!'

Ice seemed to form in Boone's stomach. Bartolome Huerta!

'Drop the gunbelt, gringo!'

Boone lowered his hands and unbuckled his gunbelt. His double-action Colt was in one of his saddlebags. He had removed his wrist clip with the derringer in it because a heat rash had formed under it during the day. It too was in his saddlebags. His only weapon was the knife he had purchased in Naco, formed from a file, slim and deadly, which he carried in a soft leather sheath in his right boot.

'Walk outside, gringo.'

Boone walked outside. He looked back over his shoulder. Dimly he saw the broad flat face, the flat reptilian eyes, thick ragged mustache, the smallpox pits. Huerta stepped back. A curved knife was in his brown hand. The deadly gutting knife; the *saca tripas*.

Boone eyed the Mexican. He had been through hell from the looks of him. The face had thinned out. His clothing was ragged and tattered. He wore no gunbelt.

Huerta grinned in the dimness. 'I saw you coming, you garbage,' he said thinly. 'There is a score we must even, pig!'

An icy trickle of sweat ran down from Boone's armpits as he eyed the dull gleam of the curved knife blade. 'Take the horse, Huerta,' he said. 'Why kill me?'

The Mexican reached up and touched the scabbed scar on his chin where the bucket thrown by Boone at Maxon's ranch had struck him. 'Son of a goat,' he said. 'Do you think I forget this?'

'Where is Bass?' asked Boone.

Huerta jerked his left hand, pointing west. 'In the hills.'

'Beyond town?'

'No. Miles from here. It is there I go when I have finished with you.'

There was a bitterness in Bartolome's tone. Boone looked closely at him. 'You got your share of the gold?'

Huerta spat.

'You have fallen out with Bass then?' asked Boone.

'Yes. The scum sent me back to scout. When I returned to the waterhole he was gone with the food and the water kegs.'

'And the gold?'

'Of course!'

'Supposing I help you trail him? You can have your share of the gold. I want the girl.'

Huerta threw back his head and laughed. 'Do you take me for such a fool?'

The bay showed at the door of the old building, looking past Huerta at Boone.

'I am not dead! I lived through the desert although my horse died. I'll follow him to Tinajas Altas and kill him. I'll take the gold and the gringa girl!'

The bay edged forward and nudged into Huerta. He jerked his head sideways. Boone closed in, smashing at Huerta's chin. Blood flew from the crusted scab. The Mexican went back against the wall, swiping at Boone with the wickedly curved *saca tripas*. It swept over his head. Boone stopped and whipped his knife free from its boot sheath.

Huerta circled swiftly, grinning with pain. This was his game. The ripping of guts. 'Ha, gringo,' he said. 'You have the guts to face me with the knife?'

'I'm here.'

Huerta's movements were sinuous and graceful, his body relaxed. The curved knife leaped in and slashed through Boone's left sleeve drawing a thin trickle of blood from the forearm. Boone retreated. Huerta moved in. The *saca tripas* lanced in but Boone leaped aside, countering with a hard thrust which Huerta easily avoided.

Their breaths came harsh in their throats. The desert had taken a bigger toll of their strength than they had realized.

Boone swung up his blade and Huerta leaped in, ripping up with the blade but his foot rolled on gravel and he staggered sideways to regain his balance. Boone's blade drew blood from Huerta's left side, just over the hip, a ragged slashing blow that drew a flow that stained Huerta's dirty shirt. He gasped as he shuffled away, weaving and swaying, watching Boone's cold eyes.

They closed. In a swift interplay of clashing blades Boone felt the *saca tripas* pink his chest before he threw the panting Mexican back. The blood stain was big on Huerta's shirt now, black in the darkness of the shadows.

Huerta moved steadily. He grunted as he thrust out his blade, trying to get the offensive, but Boone was always just out of reach. There was no doubt in his mind that Huerta was by far the better man.

Huerta tried a sweeping slash, spinning

about as he turned away, offering his broad back for an instant. Boone feinted and jumped back. The *saca tripas* swept up from below in a wicked ripping movement.

Their wrists crossed. Strength flowed from the straining bodies. Boone felt Huerta weaken. He threw him back with an upward rip of his *cuchillo*. It sank deeply, grated against bone and then was free, spraying blood against Boone's face.

Huerta coughed and moved back. There was fear on his face now, his left hand clasped to his gut. Suddenly the Mexican stopped, coughed again. The *saca tripas* clattered on the baked earth. His eyes were wide in his head.

Boone threw away his knife and balled his fists. The left caught Huerta in the gut over his left hand. The right smashed under the scabby chin, snapping back his head. Huerta's skull bounced from the wall behind him. A crushing right shredded his knuckles and pasted Huerta's lips and teeth together in a bloody mass. Huerta sank down against the wall. His breath bubbled in his throat.

Boone stepped back looking down at the wounded man. He seemed to see the thin face of Hilario Chavez before him and hear the soft voice of the informer. *'For favor, Mister Shattuck, let him die slowly, and tell him about Hilario Chavez, so that he knows I helped you. For favor?'*

'Huerta,' said Boone.

The Mexican's voice seemed to come from far away. 'Curse you!'

'Do you remember Hilario Chavez?'

'That ... *bazofa?'*

'Yes. The man whose sister you murdered. He was the one who set me on your trail.'

Huerta coughed and sagged sideways. Then he opened his mouth. Blood flooded down through his bristly beard and dripped blackly onto his dirty shirt. Then he was gone.

Boone picked up his rifle and knife. He led the bay away from the dead man, the horse shying and blowing at the smell of blood. Score three for Perry Thorne. Boone did not look back.

The *zopilotes* would take care of Bartolome Huerta.

CHAPTER NINETEEN

Two days of hell lay behind Boone. He plodded through a weird valley. To each side were tilted masses of rock, layer on layer of vari-colored stone, slanting up toward the west like the prows of half-sunken ships, half immersed in a sandy sea.

The bay was far gone, limping from innumerable cactus needles in his legs. Now and then Boone tried to remove them, bloodying the bay's legs and his hands, sometimes extracting the barbs from the horse flesh only to drive them into his own.

The valley was a maze of cacti. Barrel cactus, prickly pear, cholla, deerhorn, catclaw, elephant ear, hedgehog and fish hook. Lizards scuttled for cover at his slow approach. Hawks veered away. The trail had long since petered out on rock flats, but some animal instinct kept him moving on. The salt sweat irritated the bullet graze and knife slash on his left arm. Blisters had formed on his feet and had broken, pasting socks, feet and boots together in an aching mass. But it was the horse he worried about. He walked most of the time. The horse was used for his gear.

There were black specks in the sky. Specks that moved slowly. It was impossible to make out what they were without a glass, but Boone knew. *Zopilotes*. He had seen them hovering over Tres Jacales the day after he had left there, now and then swooping low and disappearing from sight.

There was nothing of man to be seen. Not like the trails of Arizona or Texas where a worn shoe, a scrap of dried out harness, the ashes of a fire, an empty bottle bluing in the hot sun, might be seen. Nothing.

Far ahead of him, dimly purple on the

horizon, was a rising line, as though of an island seen across many miles of a motionless sea.

He reached the end of the tip-tilted ships of the desert, the striated rock layers. He found himself trending to the right. Lost men walked in circles.

The sun was a molten blade against his neck. He pulled up his collar and buttoned it about his lean corded neck. Sweat worked down his body, pasting his shirt and under-shirt against him. A slow itching feeling came over him. He drew in a deep breath which seemed to come from an oven. He shook his head and dropped the reins of the bay. He squatted in the meager shade of the horse, wetting a rag of bandanna which he placed in his mouth, sucking the moisture from it.

'A strange land, almost unreal, as though on the moon or a distant planet. There are voices there that speak to a man's inner soul and tell him strange terrible things. A man must put his trust in God out there or lose his reason. A man is alone, yet not lonely, for he is close to God in that terrible place. Do you believe in God, my son?'

Boone raised his head. 'Yes, Father Joseph.'

'It is well. You will need Him.'

Boone jerked his head and looked over his shoulder. There was nothing behind him but the bay.

Boone stood up and gripped the reins. He plodded on, a gaunt lath of a man, his eyes slitted against the glare of the sun's rays reflecting from the whitish earth.

The wind began to rise with a hissing sound, blowing against Boone and the weak bay. Sand particles sifted down his collar, up his sleeves and into his shirt front.

There was a yellowish haze about the molten, brassy sun. A sickly color. Far ahead was a naked ledge of rock, thrusting itself up like a great knife blade from the yellow-white surface of the ground. Boone plodded on, dragging now and then at the reins. By the time they reached the ledge the desert had vanished in a haze of swirling sand.

Boone found a cleft beneath the ledge big enough for himself. The bay stood with lowered head, half in the cavity. The wind moaned like a soul in torment. Boone removed his saddle, saddlebags and canteens from the bay and stored them in the back of the cleft and settled down. The storm might blow itself out as quickly as it had come.

Boone awoke to thick darkness. He pulled the stifling blanket from his head. His boots were half buried in drifted sand. He pulled them free and crawled out into the windy night. The sand storm had died out. The moon shown faintly over the far mountains. The bay was gone.

Boone went back to his gear. He slung his canteens over his shoulder after re-filling them from the keg which had started a leak. He carried the remains of his food supply in his pockets, his Winchester in his hand. He started northwest again through the windy dimness.

The *zopilotes* had been joined by their gruesome allies, the vultures. There was little to distinguish them from each other at the great height at which they soared except for the white spots under the wings of the vultures. It didn't really matter, thought Boone, as he slogged up an incline of loose powdery sand.

He looked up to see the swiftly soaring shadow sweep down on him. He threw himself to one side as the *zopilote* shot over him. The odor of carrion hung in the still hot air of the afternoon. Boone raised his rifle and then lowered it. Spots seemed to dance before his eyes. But the spots were alive, soaring patiently. They had time. The desert was theirs.

He plodded on until at last he stood at the crest. He did not believe what he saw.

Across an area of jumbled black rock rose a steeply pitched slope of black lava. Beyond that were low mounded hills. Beyond them rose the dim mountains which had always seemed at an impossible distance for him to travel.

He slogged down the far side of the dune and entered the malpais. Jagged lava rock cut at his thin boots. Higher and higher the black rock rose until it was many feet over his head as he plodded through a labyrinthine passage. The sweat burst from his body and soaked his stinking clothing.

He rounded a turn and stopped short. A horse lay on the baking rock. It was the mount Bartolome Huerta had brought to the Kofas to meet him and Bass Eccles. They had passed that way.

It was late afternoon when he left the malpais and dropped beneath a creosote bush. His boots were in tatters. He patiently wrapped them with strips of his stinking shirt. One canteen was full. He walked on again.

The earth was all a haze, one with the sky. Joshua trees raised their gaunt hairy arms in supplication to the pitiless sky. Tortured growths of a tortured land.

Boone wiped the sweat from his face and looked west. A thread of smoke flung against the sky. Boone raised his head. Then he saw the second thread of smoke rising from a gaunt peak. A third rose from a range of hills to the north. *Yaquis.*

CHAPTER TWENTY

Boone lay prone on a rocky rise looking off into the velvet darkness to the west. Somewhere between him and the heights ahead of him must be the Yaquis. *The Bronze race that knows how to die*. He had seen two of them move across the rocky area ahead of him through the darkening shadows just after he had seen the smoke signals.

This was their country. The Sierra Madre of the North. The Apache and the Yaqui are cousins. A Yaqui mother quiets her child by saying the *yori* will get him. Not ogres or witches, but *yori* ... the *White foreigners. The Americans.* Al Sieber, the German-born Chief of Scouts for Crook, Howard and Miles, had once told Boone a Yaqui saying used by the mother of a Yaqui child. 'The *yori* killed your father. The *yori* killed your grandfather. The *yori* killed my father. Son, kill the *yori*. Never trust them.'

The desert was awakening to its nocturnal life. Yaquis were hunting *yori* and Boone was hunting Yaquis.

Boone set off slowly through the darkness, planting each foot carefully, rifle slanted across his chest; eyes, ears and nose tuned to the night sounds. Ahead of him the dim bulk of the mountains showed.

The moon showed wanly in the eastern sky when Boone caught the odor of horses. A horse whinnied softly not a hundred yards from him, upwind. Boone froze as he heard the soft padding of feet. A shadow moved across an open space. There was no mistaking the lank black hair and the loose easy stride of the Yaqui. The Yaqui vanished toward the horses.

Boone made his way through the tumbled rocks and thick brush. In half an hour he could see the faint light of the fire. Now and then the silhouette of a horse showed against the glow. Three Yaquis squatted beside it. He worked his way forward, up through rocks and boulder still hot from the day's sun.

The moon was up high when he reached a level area five hundred feet above the desert floor beneath him. The fire was concealed by a ledge of high rock.

Boone padded across the level area and looked up at an almost sheer wall of rock, broken and crumbling. Beyond it was the bulk of the rugged mountain, thrusting great gaunt shoulders into the night sky. He sipped a little water, dying for a smoke, but knowing better than to light one.

He found a great crack in the low escarpment, a fault which had been widened by tumbling rocks. He worked his way up it in darkness until he reached the top. The area before him was lit by the faint moon.

There was no movement other than the rustling of the brush. Then the odor of a horse came faintly to him. Boone placed his rifle on the ground and took out his knife. He slithered across the ground moving to a higher area. He stopped there and lay flat, testing the night.

A faint ringing sound carried clearly to Boone. The metallic sound of a shod hoof. Then Boone saw a horse's head arch against the light of the moon. A shadow moved. A tall figure appeared, gripped the horse's halter and led the animal into the darkness. The man wore a hat. A white man.

Boone slid forward down the face of the rocks and got to his feet. He worked on and stopped at the lip of a hollow. To one side a ruined rock wall showed. A naked shoulder of rock thrust into the area. Boone went to it and eased around it. There were two horses picketed back in a large opening. The moonlight picked out the dim outline of a tumbledown rock house, the doors and windows black with shadow.

One of the horses snorted and shied. The other horse whinnied sharply. The door shadow thickened. A tall man appeared with a rifle in his hands. Boone watched him. Bass Eccles.

Eccles walked to the horses and spoke quietly to them. He faded into the shadows toward the lip of the level area. Boone heard the faint clicking of rocks as the outlaw moved down the slope.

Boone walked to the slope's edge. Eccles was a hundred yards away walking toward the edge of the escarpment. Boone padded toward the ruins and flattened himself against the wall. Something moved inside. Someone was coming to the door not five feet from Boone.

A shadow appeared. Boone raised the knife. Then he lowered it. 'Marion,' he said softly.

The girl whirled and raised a pistol. The double click of the hammer sounded clearly.

'Marion! It's Boone! Boone Shattuck!'

She stood still eyeing him across the raised pistol. 'He's dead,' she said. 'Who are you?'

Boone raised his hands and stepped out into the moonlight.

She stared unbelievingly at the gaunt man who faced her, dressed in filthy undershirt and ragged trousers. She saw the hollow eyes and the thick growth of beard. Then she lowered the pistol and ran to him. He took her in his arms. The odor of sour sweat-soaked clothing filled his nostrils, but it seemed sweet to him. She clung to him. 'I don't believe it,' she whispered. 'It's impossible.'

'Are you alone with Eccles?'

'Yes. He got rid of Huerta.'

Boone looked across her shoulder. Eccles was not in sight. He led her into the dark building. 'Where are the Yaquis?'

She raised her head. 'Below us. Bass said they are in the pass behind us, too. They followed us for a full day. We rested here thinking we had shaken them off but they showed up in the afternoon.'

'How many of them?'

'We saw at least six. There may be more.'

Boots clicked on the hard earth. Boone pushed the girl back. 'Keep quiet,' he said.

Boone flattened himself against the wall. Eccles stopped outside. Then he came on and stepped into the room. 'I could see a fire,' he said to the girl. 'We can't make a break. They're probably in the pass, too.'

Boone stepped forward and placed the tip of the knife against Eccles' back. 'Stand still, Bass,' he said thinly. 'This *cuchillo* may slip if you move.'

Boone felt the tall outlaw tense. 'Shattuck.'

'Yes. You thought you killed me, Bass. You were never more wrong in your misbegotten life.'

Eccles raised his hands, still holding the rifle.

'Take the rifle, Marion,' said Boone.

She took the Winchester. Boone reached around Bass and took his two six-guns. He stepped back, cocking one of the six-guns. 'Turn around,' he said.

'For Christ's sake, Boone! Don't shoot! You'll rouse them damned bushy-headed devils.'

'They won't jump you at night. You know that.'

Eccles shifted. 'Yeh. Yeh. But they're out there like prowling wolves waitin' for dawn.'

Boone looked at the dim figure of the girl. 'What about water?'

'There's a rock pan behind the house. There's very little in it.'

'I'm going back to get my rifle,' said Boone. 'Hold this gun on him.'

Eccles tilted his head to one side. 'Look, Boone,' he said. 'I won't cause no trouble. Yuh got to help us.'

'I will, Eccles. Then you and I will have an accounting.'

'Anything you say!'

Boone walked outside and went to his rifle. He looked over the escarpment. A man stood on a rock looking toward the old ruin. A Yaqui. He vanished even as Boone watched.

Boone went back to the old house. Behind it, cracking the mountain wall, was a deep path of shadow. The pass. It wasn't very wide, a channel of darkness from which a cool night wind soughed. Boone stepped into the house with cocked rifle. Eccles was leaning against the wall. Boone walked to the corner where a dim eye of fire glowed in the beehive fireplace. He threw some wood on the fire. It flickered up He turned to look at Marion. She was thin with privation, her eyes hollow in her face. Eccles squatted by the fire. He looked up at Boone. 'What do we do?' There was undisguised fear in his voice.

Boone lowered the hammer on his rifle. 'Sit tight until before dawn. Then we'll go after them.'

'We're better off here!'

'With a dozen of them waiting? You ever fought Indians?'

'No.'

'Well, they don't take chances. They'd never rush you.'

'I don't like it!'

'They don't know I'm here.'

'Then you go!'

Boone felt for the makings and rolled a smoke. 'What were you trying to do up here? Kill yourself and the girl?'

Eccles wiped his face. 'Chacon knew I was back in Sonora. They followed us to Pitiquito. I couldn't go south. He has men operatin' clear down to Soyopa. The Rurales were lookin' for me in the Sierra Vallecillos on a tip. I figgered I'd fox them all by headin' west on the Camino del Diablo.'

'Heading for where?'

Eccles squatted on the floor letting his long

arms dangle over his bony knees. 'Maybe San Luis. Gulf steamers come up there to discharge cargo for the Colorado River steamers.'

'You'd be spotted right away.'

'Maybe. Anyways I figgered I'd head for Ensenada and get a coastal steamer outa there headin' for Mazatlan, Tuxpan or maybe even Panama.'

'Your money won't pay your way through the Yaquis.'

Eccles bowed his bald head. 'Yeh.'

'Wells-Fargo may have men in San Luis.'

'I've foxed Wells-Fargo. I ain't worried about them.'

'That so?'

Eccles head snapped up. 'What do you mean?'

'Nothing.'

Eccles rolled a smoke and lit it with shaking hands.

Boone leaned back against the wall. Marion was in bad shape. Her eyes never left Boone. 'Why is Chacon after you?'

Eccles took the cigarette from his cracked lips. 'I offered him a split. Bartolome told me Chacon figgered on taking the whole kit and caboodle.'

'Diamond cut diamond, eh?'

'What the hell does that mean?'

Boone grinned. 'Takes a thief to rob a thief.'

'To Hell with this loco talk! How do we get out of this mess?'

Boone stood up. 'Before dawn I'll leave here, find a good shooting place. You and Marion will have to hold this place. Can they get behind you?'

'Down the pass.'

'I'll cover that too.'

Eccles rolled another smoke. 'You help me get out of this, Boone, and I'll split.'

'*You?* I'm thinking about her.'

Eccles looked up. 'We're all in it now.'

'Where's the gold?'

Eccles jerked his head. 'In the corner.'

Boone looked at the full ticking sacks. 'If we have to pull foot we'll leave it behind.'

Eccles jumped to his feet. 'Not on your life!'

Boone grinned. 'It may mean *your* life.'

Marion stood up. 'Don't go out there, Boone. He isn't to be trusted.'

Boone went to her. 'He'll have to stick with us. Yaquis have some clever ways of torturing white men. I don't think Bass wants to be the subject of one of them.'

Bass cringed. 'I'll play the game.'

Boone handed the girl his rifle. 'Are you tired?'

'I couldn't sleep, Boone.'

'Then watch him while I get some sleep. I'll need it.' He stooped and kissed her cracked lips.

'Very touching,' jeered Eccles.

Boone dropped on the floor and placed an arm across his burning eyes. He went to sleep instantly.

CHAPTER TWENTY-ONE

Boone looked up into Marion's dim face. 'It will be dawn soon,' she said.

Boone shivered in the cold. She handed him a cup of coffee. 'This is the last,' she said.

'You take it.'

She shook her head.

Boone sipped the strong brew. Eccles was asleep in the corner with his head resting on the plump ticking sacks. 'How did he treat you?' asked Boone.

She leaned her head back against the wall. 'All right. He never touched me until we came up here.'

Boone lowered the cup. 'What happened then?'

She placed a hand on his arm. 'He thought we were safe. Last night he tried to make love to me. He promised me everything if I would.'

'So?'

She touched the front of her clothing. It

had been ripped from neck to waistline and roughly pinned together with thorns. 'I couldn't fight anymore. Then we heard the horses neigh. He went to look and saw the Yaquis. He forgot all about me then.'

Boone eyed the sleeping outlaw.

She drew a blanket about her shoulders. 'Do you think we can get away, Boone?'

'Yes,' he lied.

Boone stood up and took the Winchester. 'I'll leave now. Keep out of sight. Shoot only if they rush you.' He lifted her face with his free hand. 'You must remember something.'

'Yes,' she said quietly.

He picked up her Colt and checked the cylinder. 'There are six cartridges in here.' He placed the heavy gun in her slim brown hands. 'You must save one for yourself if necessary. Do you understand?'

She looked down at the Colt. 'Are you trying to say goodbye to me, Boone?'

'No. But do not let them take you alive.'

Boone left. It was still dark, a whispering darkness, the wind moaning softly through the pass and rustling the brush. He padded to a place where he could see both the lip of the escarpment and the pass. He could cover the level area in front of the ruined building. He dropped to the ground and lay still. He wondered who had ever built such a place.

The sky lightened almost imperceptibly in

212

the East. It was cold. Boone half-cocked his rifle. He had twelve rounds in it. He drew out his two Colts and loaded the empty cylinder chambers on which the hammer normally rested. Twelve more rounds. He touched the derringer clipped under his undershirt sleeve. Two rounds. One for himself if they broke through on him.

It grew lighter. Boone stared at a bushy head for minutes before he realized it was a bush instead of a Yaqui. Somewhere, high in the dark pass, an eagle screamed. It was answered from below the escarpment. Almost a perfect imitation. A set feeling came over Boone. Kill or be killed.

Two *yori* were at the old ruin. A man and a woman. The man might die quickly or be saved for torture. The woman would be used until she was a screaming, thrashing wreck on the ground. War the Yaqui way.

Silently through the brush they came.

One minute the escarpment was empty. The next minute three shadowy figures were there, slipping toward a pile of scattered rock. Something moved in the pass. Two more.

Boone wet his dry lips. He eased the Winchester forward. There was no movement at the house. Boone's heart thudded against his ribs.

Another Yaqui showed beyond the house, standing behind a tall bush. Now the sky was lighter. Ready for the swift, deadly rush on silent feet.

The three Yaquis behind the rocks stood up. Boone rested his cheek against the scarred stock of the rifle. He took up the trigger slack. He squeezed off. The rifle spat and pushed back against his shoulder. He levered another round home, sighted and fired again before the echoes died away on the rock face. One Yaqui was down. The second thrashed about. The third was staring at Boone's position. The slug took him fair on the breastbone driving him back over his two mates.

Boone turned. A Yaqui was scuttling for cover in the pass. Boone fired. The impact of the heavy slug drove the buck forward on his knees. The second slug plowed into his back.

Two warriors bounded from the brush trying to reach the escarpment. A rifle flashed from a window. One of them went down. The other stumbled over him. Another bullet sent him to the House of Spirits.

Six down. Boone reloaded. Smoke drifted across the level area. The horses screamed like frightened women. One of them jerked back. His picket pin flew through the air and clattered on the hard earth. He buck-jumped toward the escarpment, crashing through the brush. A Yaqui jumped out of his way. Eccles and Boone fired simultaneously. The Yaqui sprawled in death. The frenzied horse plunged down the escarpment in a rattle of stones and gravel, striking hard far below.

The echoes died away. The Eastern sky was light, bringing into relief the sharp crags of the eastern mountains.

One of the Yaquis thrashed about, his legs locked from a shattered spine. Boone stood up and walked forward. Eccles came out of the house. He walked to the Yaqui and fired at three feet. Bits of hair and skull flew away from the smash of the soft-nosed slug.

Boone looked down the escarpment. Three Yaquis were riding fast away from the base of the steep slope. Boone pumped his Winchester dry after them, forcing them to scatter. It was all over.

Eccles grinned. 'We did it,' he said.

Boone nodded. 'One horse left. Marion can ride him.'

Eccles' face tightened. 'What about the gold?'

'We'll bury it.'

'Hell no! It goes.'

Boone threw aside his Winchester and dropped his hand to his Colt. The holster was empty. Then he remembered he had left both of his six-guns lying back at his position.

Marion came out of the house and ran to Boone. 'Thank God.'

Boone looked across her shoulder at Eccles. The tall outlaw held his Winchester at hip level pointing toward them. His face looked like a death's-head. 'Get away from the woman,' he said thinly.

Boone gently pushed her back.

'Get into the house,' said Eccles.

Boone walked toward the house. He stepped in. Eccles prodded him in the back with the rifle. A cold trickle of sweat worked down Boone's sides.

'Stand in the corner with your back to me,' said Eccles. 'Get them hands up high.'

'He saved our lives!' called Marion.

'Shut up! Get that hoss.'

She led the horse to the front of the house. 'Get them money sacks. Tie 'em onto the horse.' She did as she was told.

Eccles stepped back. 'The canteens are full,' he said. 'Marion, you lead that horse up the pass.'

'No!'

'Git! Git, or I'll shoot.'

She came closer to Bass. 'Let him go and I'll go with you.'

'Git!'

She led the horse past the house, the hoofs clashing on the gravel.

Boone stared at the wall. His hands were up high. He hoped to God Eccles didn't notice the bulge at his left wrist under the filthy undershirt sleeve.

'You and me might have gone places together, Shattuck. We'd of made a good team.'

216

Boone almost reached for the derringer.

Eccles spat. 'I guess I'm just a lobo,' he said. 'I like to make you poor bastards work for me and then take the loot.'

'You haven't a chance, Eccles.'

'I've done all right so far.'

'Yes.'

Eccles shifted. He cocked the rifle.

Boone spoke over his shoulder. 'I'll make a deal,' he said.

'Go to hell!'

'Listen, Bass. Wells-Fargo knows you've come this way. They wired ahead to Yuma. They have agents from Yuma down to San Luis. You can't go south, Chacon is ravaging the country.'

'How do you know?' There was fear in his voice.

Boone thought quickly. 'A Wells-Fargo man was at Naco.'

'You're a damned liar!'

'I waylaid him and took his badge and credentials. They're in my pocket.'

'Turn around.'

Boone turned to face the muzzle of the rifle. There was fear in Eccles' dark eyes.

'Reach down easylike,' said Bass. 'Get them credentials.'

Boone slid his right hand into his pocket and took out the badge and the folded paper. He handed them to Eccles. Eccles held the rifle in his right hand, finger pressing against the trigger. He glanced down at the badge. 'Yeh. This is the real thing.' He fumbled with the paper and unfolded it. He read the name on it and his eyes widened.

Boone kicked out. The Winchester barrel went up and the gun roared. Eccles cursed and jumped back. Boone gripped the barrel in his left hand and forced it up. Eccles smashed a fist at Boone's face. The blow half-stunned him. He went back against the wall. Eccles let go of the rifle and jumped back, clawing for his Colt.

Boone ripped the derringer from its clip and cocked it as Eccles' Colt came up. Both weapons roared. Something slammed Boone back against the wall. He went down and rolled away as Eccles fired again. The slug screamed from the packed earth floor.

Boone's right shoulder was numb. He jerked the derringer with his left hand from his right and fired from the noon.

Eccles jerked, staggered back. His eyes were glazing even as he fired for the last time. The Colt dropped from nerveless fingers as Eccles hit the wall and slid to the floor over the ticking sacks. He opened his mouth and a flood of blood poured from it, soaking into the sacks.

Boone bent his head and touched his own right shoulder. His hand came away stained with blood. The slug had plowed just over the bone, cutting a deep furrow. His gut moiled.

'Boone!' Marion stood in the doorway. She looked at Eccles and then ran to Boone, cradling him in her arms. 'You're hurt bad!'

He looked up at her. Her eyes were wet. 'It's all over, isn't it, Boone?'

'Yes. We'll rest awhile. Then head for Yuma.'

She touched his gaunt face. 'And then?'

He grinned. 'Why we'll head for Texas, honey. Where else?'

She kissed him hard. He drew her close with his left arm and then suddenly forgot the pain in his right shoulder as he crushed her to him, feeling the softness of her. The bloody trail of death was over. A new life would begin for the two of them. The hate was out of him now. The desert had burned the impurities out of him. Somewhere on the desert below them a thrasher lifted its rich song to greet the morning sun.

The publishers hope that this book has given you enjoyable reading. Large Print Books are especially designed to be as easy to see and hold as possible. If you wish a complete list of our books please ask at your local library or write directly to:

The Golden West Large Print Books
Magna House, Long Preston,
Skipton, North Yorkshire.
BD23 4ND